Epsilon

Dezirae Bates

BLUE FORGE PRESS

Port Orchard ✿ Washington

Dedication

For Joseph, Amelia, and Benjamin.

The Origins
Book 1

Epsilon

Dezirae Bates

Chapter 1

ad, Dad, yes, I'm leaving work now, alright? Yeah—
ju-just stay there, okay? I'll be there in about five
minutes," Cassidy said over the tone of music
behind her, the beat of the melody streaming out amongst
the crowd as she exited the bar. For a Wednesday night, the
bar was overwhelmed with guests and had she not pulled a
double the night before, her boss probably wouldn't have let
her leave early at all.

"Excus- please, excuse me!" Cassidy bellowed, pushing
her way through the crowds before finally reaching her car. it
was rather small, not too fancy or new but it got her from
point A to B. A quick scramble through her purse produced a
handful of keys, jingling as they found their home in the door
of her car. Seconds ticked by, the car revving to life once the
ignition flipped over.

It'd been a long time since she had to pick her father up,
drunk, in a bar. Jack had yet to drink to this level since after

her mother died, exactly a year ago today. The biggest thing that Cassidy was thankful for was that he called her instead of taking the drive home himself.

"Hey Bernie," she muttered, nodding towards the man near the front of the door, his expression lightening at the sight of her.

"He's in his spot, kinda loud tonight too," he warned, opening the door for her as she slipped in, heading straight for the far back stool.

"Cassidy!" Jack exclaimed, hiccuping for a moment, his words slurring as he lifted his head up to meet his daughter's gaze.

"Yeah, hi Dad, nice to see you too," she said with a bit of a cough, sliding his stool away from the bar and helping him, a little uneasily, to his feet and trying to edge him out of the bar one foot at a time.

"I'll settle the rest in the morning," Cassidy said, mid sigh, as she slid the handful of cash she had in her pocket, giving him a hopefully forgivable smile as she headed back to her car.

"Dad... you can't keep doing this to yourself, you know," she started as she backed out of the spot, heading down the more rural roads towards her father's home.

"Don't start, Cass," he mumbled, clasping his hand over his face and trying to prevent himself from getting sick all over the glove box, swallowing down the urge as best he could.

And, instead of getting into with him, she took a gentle sigh, nodded her head and leaned back in her seat, trying to focus on the musical lull as she drove to her childhood home.

Each road gave way to the next, twisting and turning their way through the town. Over the course of the past fifteen minutes, a total of two cars managed to pass them. To say they lived in a town that closed down when the sun set was an understatement. Despite the fact that the bars had fairly frequent customers, everything else became a ghost town.

Cassidy was barely four minutes away when the startling

bright lights of an oncoming car headlights shone in her eyes. By this point, her father was fast asleep, snoring loudly in her passenger seat and content to start the sleep off now rather than later. Cassidy squinted through the sudden burst of light and wouldn't have had any problem with them other than the fact that while the cars were quickly growing closer, the other vehicle began to swerve into her lane.

"Come on, asshole," she muttered, laying on her horn which only seemed to increase the other vehicle's speed and before she knew it, the vehicle she was controlling veered far off the road, far more than she had anticipated and broke through the stone barrier bridge. Her stomach leapt into her chest, the metal crunching sound resonating into her ears as she braced her body for impact.

"Shit!" she exclaimed, her knuckles ghost white as they gripped tighter onto the steering wheel. The car seemed to float through the air, seconds taking what felt like years to connect with the water below. Lake Holiday's waterline was much higher than normal for the time of year, mainly due to the great influx of rain for the region. Many townsfolk were worried it would flood several times over the past few weeks but Cassidy never seemed to care. Well, she didn't care, until now.

The thud that came from the car as it crashed into the water was only masked by the scream that tore from Cassidy's throat. Her head slammed forward, feet suddenly cold while her face was increasingly warm. She could feel the sticky red substance rolling down between her cheek and her nose, making its way to the edge of her lips before the metallic taste flooded her senses. The haze that fell over her head was instantaneous and was quickly followed by a headache she could only describe as being unbearable. Black spots floated around in her vision causing her to blink several times even just to focus. Pain radiated from her knee, her jeans torn from where the car had thrown her forward and breathing was becoming more and more difficult with each breath. Despite everything, those were the least of her concerns. Currently, her mind was trained on one thing: the fact that the water that was once on her feet was now near her thigh.

"Dad!" she screamed, her fingers clawing around at her seatbelt clip, desperate to free herself. While one hand messed with the buckle, her other was shaking her father's arm as best she could, screaming out his name as she tried to free herself. A few more shakes of his arm and it was obvious that she wasn't going to be able to wake him from the way she was seated. Getting herself out first would be the only way.

"Let me out!" she said in frustration, pulling and yanking at the fabric that was supposed to save her life but was now binding her to her car like a coffin. At this point, the water was close to the buckle itself and with one final pull, the belt freed her.

A quick reach over to her father's buckle resulted in the same issue she had with her own. It was as if the buckle had a mind of its own.

"Dad, Dad, Dad!!!" she screamed, trying to shake him sober for just a minute to help. The water continued to rise, now to their chests as she finally heard the click of the seat belt unbuckle. Finally.

Every breath she took up until now was simply to free herself from the car but now, the vehicle was almost completely submerged. The inside of the vehicle wasn't pressurized enough for her to open the door under the water and she wasn't strong enough to kick out a window.

She screamed out for help, pleading for someone, anyone, to come and help her. When the water reached up to her mouth, a few last ditch grabs managed to pry the door open. A quick breath filled her lungs, a whimper leaving her throat at the pain of breathing so deep caused. Glancing at her father who was almost completely submerged and still unconscious, Cassidy tried to pull the slack of the seatbelt off of him. Gliding through the water brought up the pain in her knee, finally trying to move it for the first time which made her open her mouth to scream. The pain was so indescribable that she would rather lose her last breath she had than not scream.

Cassidy was at a crossroads. Helping her father would inevitably kill her as the amount of time should could survive without a breath was limited. Swimming up to the surface, however painful it might be, would at least give her another bit of air and perhaps enough energy to swim back down and retrieve her father from the depths of the lake. She had to make a decision.

Cassidy pushed herself past her father, her gut retching at the idea of leaving him to die instead of saving him. Looking to the surface, she couldn't ascertain how deep the lake actually was but the fact that she couldn't see any light from above told her she had a lot of swimming to do. She pushed on, willing herself to swim harder and faster, a trail of blood flowing after her as she persisted. She closed her eyes as the pain started to take over, not only from her leg but from her head as well.

It took but a second for her to lose consciousness, her hair flowing in the water around her body as her heart began to slow.

Cassidy Hawkins was dead. But, for the first time in her life, she was alive.

Chapter 2

The room was frigid, a constant beep from the monitor practically sang to her as she laid in the hospital bed. Cassidy was going on hour seven of unconsciousness, a large bandage covering her forehead, IV bag hooked up into her arm, and her knee set in a brace. The clothes she'd been wearing earlier were traded in for a gray hospital gown. A small vase of yellow sunflowers perched next to her on the desk, a card saying something to the effect of "Get Well Soon" sprawled across the top. The light seemed to get brighter as the seconds ticked by and the need to wake up forced Cassidy to open her eyes .

Cassidy groaned, trying desperately to sit up in the bed but, even through the medicine, the pain hit her like a brick wall. Breathing was difficult but not impossible and adjusting her weight in her bed wasn't going to be happening anytime soon with her leg.

"I wouldn't move too much if I were you," a voice echoed,

entering the room as Cassidy lifted her gaze to the man. He was wearing a navy blue henley shirt, jeans, Chucks and his brown hair on top was rather short but still had room to play with it if he cared to. She squinted at him for a minute, letting her eyes try and figure out if she knew him at all, which she didn't.

"Where's my Dad?" she said, pushing herself up in her seat as best she could and pulling the blanket up over her legs to cover herself. The man didn't have any signs of being a doctor and the fact that she didn't recognize him but he was in her room caused a shiver of fear to rise in her chest.

The stranger's calm demeanor changed ever so slightly as his smile became a grimace, his tongue running over his bottom lip before clasping his hands together. "You don't know yet?" he asked, glancing over his shoulder at the doctors who were flipping through her chart, speaking to an older gentleman in a suit and completely ignoring Cassidy.

"Know what?" she asked, attempting to shift her weight and lean forward, the sharp breath that she took in burned her lungs and forced out a cough. "Who are you? Just, let me see my Dad," she started, trying to reach for the IV in her arm to rip it out, the heartbeat monitor alarming as she tried.

"Miss Hawkins, please, we need you to remain calm," a doctor said, standing next to the stranger. He was roughly five foot five, somewhat plump and appeared to be trying to calm her down, as best he could.

Cassidy stopped struggling when the doctor stepped in, glancing from the stranger, her heart still racing. "I'm calm... Can someone just tell me where my Dad is?" she asked, a bit of anger creeping up inside her before setting her eyes on the doctor himself.

"I'm sorry, Miss Hawkins. Your father—he was injured in the crash and while you were already out of the car when Mr. Williams here got to you, you were easier to retrieve. If it wasn't for his quick actions, you might not be with us."

He paused, glancing to her chart before looking back up at

her to continue. "By the time he learned there was another in the car, your father had already been submerged too long. I'm sorry," he said, his voice as soothing as he could muster in the moment.

Cassidy had assumed when the stranger skirted around the question that something dreadful had happened but she didn't anticipate it being his death. She did everything she could to pull him out of the car.

The tears edged over her eyes and she tried to blink them away, swallowing back the sob as best she could as she brought her hands to her eyes and wiped them from her face. Her eyes closed, clutching them shut for a moment as her shoulders shuddered, trying not to blame herself for not getting there in time. It took her a moment or two before she glanced up at the doctor, unsure of what to say to him.

"Wha- what do I need to do?" she whispered, clearing her throat to stop herself from sounding weak and the doctor cracked a half smile, surprised at her resilience.

"Well, we've taken scans of your brain and it appears to be a bad concussion. We'd like to monitor you for the night, see how your headaches go and check over your lungs. You'd been out for about thirty seconds before he was able to pull you out," he said, nodding to Chase who's arms were crossed over his chest.

"I'm just glad I saw you go off. And was able to get to you in time," he said, running his hand over the scruff of his jaw as Cassidy stared.

"So, you're saying I was dead? Legitimately, for thirty seconds or so?" she asked, clearing her throat again, rubbing away the burning pain as Chase quickly grabbed her a glass of water and handed it over.

"Doc said your heart stopped for a few seconds. Another minute or so down there and you wouldn't have made it at all." Chase nodded, Cassidy quietly thanking him for the glass of water as she sucked it down.

"Guess I should thank you," she mumbled, not meeting his

gaze as she looked back at the doctor.

"We'll let you rest for now, the nurses will be by in a bit. You can let them know if you have any pain or discomfort, they'll try to make you comfortable," he said, glancing to Chase for a minute before turning on his heel and leading out the room.

Chase stood for a few seconds, glancing from her flowers to Cassidy, to the floor and back up to her. He cleared his throat and shoved his hands in his pockets before speaking.

"I guess, well, you're in good hands now. Ill see ya around. I'm sorry, bout your dad," he said, not waiting for her to speak again before heading out of the room and leaving Cassidy by herself.

Chapter 3

The funeral went as well as could be expected. Most of the town—actually close to all of the town given the fact that it wasn't the largest of places—showed up. Jack might've had his issues but he was a man who was beloved by his town and his daughter. After all, he was all the family she had left.

Cassidy had fairly consistent headaches since being discharged. The concussion was the primary reason for the pain but so was the entire planning process for the funeral, burying her father and mounting the task of surviving the world without him. She'd already given up her tiny apartment at the edge of town to live in her childhood home which was far too large for just her but it was home. It was where she was brought home from the hospital, where she had her first kiss, senior prom... where every memory that made her originated from. She couldn't just leave it empty.

Today was her first day back at the bar since her accident.

Her boss was fairly understanding, giving her whatever time she needed but Cassidy needed to keep her hands and mind busy. It was the only way to survive the grief that was welling up inside her.

The doctors were surprised her leg had healed as quickly as it had, a small brace covering just her knee was necessary to stand on it for long periods of time. The hospital had thought she had extensive damage to it but as the xrays proved, she has merely strained the tendons holding it all together.

She had on a pair of black shorts that covered close to mid thigh, black tennis shoes and a blue tank top with the words Charlie's emblazioned across the chest. Her shoulder length hazelnut hair was pulled up into a rather messy bun, a few fly away curls framing her face. A quick glance at herself in the mirror caused her to sigh, her blue eyes even more blue due to the blue shirt she was wearing. "You look like death warmed over," she muttered to herself, running her fingers under her eyes, trying desperately to wipe away the circles that took up home there. To no avail, she shrugged, adjusting one of her bra straps before heading downstairs.

"Ruca," she called out, a chocolate labrador poked her head out from under the dining room table, quickly following out after Cassidy and heading to her dish. Tail wagging to and fro, Ruca whined before Cassidy was even able to open the pantry to feed her.

"Okay, I get it, I get it," she said with a gentle laugh, grabbing up a cup of the dog's food and tossing it into the silver bowl. She picked up the water bowl as Ruca started to chow down, filling up the bowl to about halfway as a quick rap echoed against the front door. Cassidy jumped, still on edge from the accident and the fact that she wasn't expecting anyone caused the reaction as well. Her head had snapped up to the door, glancing away from the water. If she'd been looking at the faucet in front of her, she'd have noticed that the water stopped mid air from continuing to flow when she was startled by the door.

It wasn't the first time that water seemed to react while being around her. Cassidy chalked it up to her being skiddish around water after nearly drowning to death but there was definitely something else that was causing the sudden change in water. And, if Cassidy were being honest with herself, she might have figured it out before the knock came upon her door.

"C-Coming," she called out, reaching out and turning the water off to the faucet and setting Ruca's bowl down on the ground, grabbing up a towel to dry her hands off as she made it to the front door. A quick peak into the peephole discovered that it was Chase Williams, the man who had saved her from drowning in the first place. She hadn't seen him since he left her in the hospital.

"Hey, how- how did you know where I live?" she asked, before he could get a word out to explain why he was there.

Chase's eyebrow shot up at her accusatory tone, shifting his weight on the balls of his feet before a short laugh escaped his lips. "Uh, small town? Your address was in the funeral announcement for your Dad. I just thought—that I'd come by and check out how you were doing," he said, glancing over her shoulder to spot Ruca finishing her food. Cassidy shifted over, blocking the rest of his view to the house behind her, clearing her throat as she looked him over.

"Oh, right, well, uh, I'm good. I mean, I'm okay. Considering," she said, pursing her lips together and giving a gentle shrug. "I'm actually about to head into work so if that was all you came by to talk about…" She trailed off, one hand on the door and she went to close it. It wasn't that she was a rude person, she just had issues trusting random strangers, even strangers who saved her life.

Chase nodded his head, feeling the cold shoulder coming from her and letting it not set into his head. He had a purpose in being here and she needed to listen to him, whether she liked it or not.

"Right, well, I need to talk to you about some stuff, regarding that night, and I think, if you could spare the time, you should give me a listen." Chase shifted once more, looking away from Cassidy and towards all the area around her. He stared at the front door, the porch, over near the bushes and back to where Ruca was now sitting a few feet behind Cassidy, presumptively protecting her from a distance. It was clear as day that the dog was unsettled. Cassidy could feel the bit of tension in the air rising, swallowing back the suddenly uncomfortable wave in the air.

"Uh- yeah, now's not really a good time," she said, glancing back at Ruca for a moment who had edged a step or two closer, trying to be within striking distance if need be. Her grip on the door strengthened, glancing from Chase to the bushes over to the edge of the porch. She could feel her heart throbbing in her chest, the blood pumping so fast that her cheeks were growing warmer and warmer. "I think you should go," she finally finished, moving to close the door in his face but Chase's arm went to stop her, easily stopping the woman from closing it on him.

"Cassidy, I'm not here to hurt you. You just need to trust me. Let me in," he said, glancing from over his shoulder back to Cassidy. Before he could plead with her once more, a stunningly green light whipped across the porch, an intense wind following with it. The stray hairs on Cassidy's head spiraled out of control around her head and where Chase once stood, he was now a decent ten feet away. It was as if a tornado had came and ripped him from her porch.

"Chase!" she exclaimed, glancing to where the light came from and spotting a blonde woman, probably a few years younger than Cassidy, around eighteen or nineteen, a pulsing green crossing over the tips of her fingers. She could feel her jaw drop at the sight of some kind of light show over the woman's hands.

Chase quickly got to his feet, disoriented for a moment before finding the blonde in the bushes to the side of

Cassidy's home.

"Geneva, you have no business being here," he snapped, a quick red light shooting from the top of his hand which moved the porch swing and hurled it towards Geneva faster than Cassidy could blink. Geneva matched Chase faster than he anticipated, a green burst simply moving the swing out of her way.

"Getting predictable in your old age, I see," she laughed, glancing from Chase to Cassidy. "We found her first, back off, wave the white flag and let us have her, Williams." She said, moving a foot or two closer to Cassidy's front door.

"And let a leech take her? There's no chance in hell. Besides, you didn't get to her first. She's joined to me. So, if you think I'm just going to let you take her, you're dead wrong." A quick smirk rose over his features, glancing from Cassidy to Geneva, a whoosh of sharp red light enveloping around him and pulsing as it teleported him from where he was to directly in front of Cassidy.

"Invite me in," he said quickly, glancing at Geneva who's green pulse started to grow as the wind began to whip around her. Cassidy still was processing the fact that he moved in front of her without actually walking, Ruca snarling behind her at the rukus outside.

"Now, Cassidy!" he exclaimed, Cassidy nodding her head and quickly giving him an invitation and he moved into the door frame, a thin vale dropping over the house after the invitation was extended as a sort of protection. Geneva cursed slightly under her breath, moving within visual distance of the doorframe and dropped the pulse of green around her hands.

"You can't keep her locked in there forever, Williams. Joined or not, there are ways to break that bond," Geneva cried out, looking Chase over before looking to Cassidy. "He's got a cute face but that's about it. Don't fall for everything that boy tells ya," she said, giving her as best of a warning she could before the green light and wind wrapped around her and she was gone before Cassidy could speak a word.

"What the hell was that?! And you, what are you?!" Cassidy exclaimed, swallowing hard as she backed herself up to the wall behind her, grasping an umbrella by the door and wielding it in front of her.

Chase placed his hands up in the air, a brief laugh leaving his lips at her attempt to protect herself from him by using an umbrella. "Don't worry, I'm not here to hurt you, like I already said. I'm here to help. And to explain. Plus, what are you gonna do with that?" He asked, the red leaving his fingers and calling the umbrella to his hands, twirling it around before setting the tip against the ground and leaning against it.

Cassidy's heart was still on fire, pumping all of the blood in her system faster than she ever thought possible as she looked him over. He literally seemed to be oozing a sort of hubris that only came along when men were used to getting their way. Her eyes narrowed at his demeanor, greatly unimpressed with his attitude before grabbing up the other umbrella in the holder by the door and holding it up to face him.

"Useless or not, it's staying right here in my hands," she said, her voice firm as she looked him over. "Now, answer my damn questions or get out of my house," she repeated, trying to hide the fact that her hands were shaking.

Chase had to be impressed that someone lacking the ability to ward him off was so keen on trying but he could sense her fear more than anyone else. He took a few steps back and sat on the arm of the couch.

"Well, what you saw was magic. The real stuff. Not the crap you see in movies or tv. As real as you and me, magic." He glanced to his fingers and watched as the red spark moved eagerly over his fingertips, a warm smile crossing his features. "And I am—well, it's hard to explain if you don't know all the information so I guess this goes back to the 'you need to trust me' bit from earlier. It's easier if I show you rather than tell you. Think you could come and have a listen?" he asked, arching a brow and crossing his arms over his chest, waiting for her answer.

"Show me? You really think I'm going to go anywhere with you after all of that? You're pushing it just being here," she said, angrily, more and more furious that her questions weren't getting answered.

"And you think you're safe here? The leeches know where you live. Geneva is right. You're not going to stay here forever so you can either come with me and I can lead you down the rabbit hole of information oooor you can stay here and just wait for them to give up looking for you. Your choice," he shrugged.

Cassidy hated ultimatums. Or, at least, she hated being placed in them. She just wanted to know why they were looking for her. Why in the world did she have anything to do with this whole mess. And, it seemed, the only way to get that information answered was to follow Chase and give him a minute to show her what was going on.

"Fine. I'll go. But, I swear to God, if something happens..." She trailed off, Chase tossing his hands up in the air to stop her from continuing.

"Don't worry, couldn't hurt ya even if I wanted to, promise," he said, crossing his fingers across his chest as he stood in front of her. "I'm gonna need your hands," he said, holding his out as Cassidy set the umbrella down and rolled her eyes slightly. "Don't worry, I don't bite," he said with a grin as Ruca growled at him. "Settle Ruca, I'll be back soon," Cassidy said to her dog, taking a hesitant breath before putting her hands in his. It only took a second for the bright red light to rope around them, first at their hands and then all over their bodies. The energy was warm and electrifying, making the hairs on Cassidy's arms spark all over as they moved from her living room to a rather ornate building. She felt slightly queezy, swallowing back the dizzy feeling as best she could before letting go of Chase's hands.

The walls were lined with books, the air smelled of an old

library and it made Cassidy feel oddly soothed. There were a few candles lit in the room and a dim light fixture in the center of the room but other than that, it was rather dark. There was a man, an older gentleman, seated in a rather ornate chair behind a desk at the far back of the room. It only took her a moment to recognize where Cassidy had seen him before. It was the man who was speaking to the doctors at the hospital after her accident.

"Hello Cassidy, I hope Chase was able to retrieve you without any major issues," he said, a warm smile fell over his lips before looking to Chase who shrugged.

"Leeches but, we're here in one piece. Even witha few minutes to spare," he said, glancing at his watch as he sat down at the table next to him. The Chancellor sighed, shaking his head at Chase before looking back to Cassidy.

"Well, you're here now and that's all that matters. Cassidy Hawkins, welcome to the Exodus.

Chapter 4

Cassidy had absolutely no idea what was going on in the moment. All she thought today was going to be about was bartending a bit, possibly dodging a drunkard or two and accepting condolences. But now, now she was facing something way over her head.

"Ohkaaay," Cassidy said, laughing softly at the rather lavish introduction of the word *Exodus*, trying not to feel like she was in the Matrix or some other alternate universe for the moment. "You mind telling me what that means or are you just gonna have me google the word and see what I get? I'm thinking lots of bible references," she said, shoving her hands into her pockets. Chase chuckled, shaking his head as he glanced to the Chancellor. "Hey, you just said I had to bring her here, not that she had to be compliant or informed. I thought that was your job with the whole 'welcome to the Exodus' thing. Far fancier than what I had drummed up," he laughed, the Chancellor's face not showing the humor in it by any frame of the imagination. Chase's smile dropped and he swallowed hard, settling back into his chair and shutting up instead of digging his hole even deeper.

"As I said, this, where you are, where Chase has brought you, is called the Exodus. The fact that you ran into some trouble on your way here means you've at least seen some aspects of our work here. Or, at least abilities," he said, offering her a chair to sit as he leaned against the back of the desk. Cassidy waved off the chair, refusing to sit until her questions were finally answered.

"He said he'd show me the answer to my questions. I was just attacked by some blonde chick on my front porch. So, if we could skip the how do you dos and just get on with it, I'd appreciate it," she said, licking her lips in frustration as the Chancellor nodded. "Sure thing," he said, rolling up his sleeves to show off the small quarter sized blotch on his left forearm.

"This is what brings you here," he said, pointing to his on his arm and then pointing to her foot, already knowing where her mark was. "We call it a signet. It's a brand, of sorts. When magical folk are born, they have this mark somewhere on them and it lies dormant until triggered. Once triggered, it activates the magical blood inside you," he said, pausing for a moment. "And, that's where we come in. The Exodus is a home for magical people, like yourself, who've become triggered and need guidance. We're the home away from home, the elders, the beginning and end for many members of this community." Cassidy moved to the seat that was previously offered to her as he spoke, knowing that she'd need the support to accept everything he was saying.

"Years ago, we were founded once we found out there were more than just a handful of us. And then, the structure came when we all started talking to one another. Each story of the signet getting triggered was different but one simple element remained constant. Death. The only way to trigger the signet on your body was for you to die, like you did when you drowned in that lake before Chase jumped in after you."

The Chancellor paused as Chase looked over to Cassidy, cracking a somewhat genuine smile.

"We've discovered over the years that there are five origins of magic, all routed in different parts of a person's soul. Each Origin is completely unique to you, personally, and connects you to the group as a whole. First there is Omicron, which is a healing Origin. Those that end up there have various abilities in one's lifesource. Their magic is branded in blue. Next is Epsilon, which is an elemental Origin. Those who find themselves in Epsilon have abilities in fire, water, earth, wood and metal and as you saw with Geneva who is a powerful elemental, their magic is rooted in green. Then you have Chi, which is where Chase finds himself. Chis are powerful telekinetics, being able to use a vast range of mental abilities and whose magic is branded in red. There's Sigma, which is connected to Necromancy, or the ability to control and aide the dead. Mediums, manipulation of life sources, they're the equal opposites to Omicrons and are branded by orange magic. And finally, there is Delta, which finds itself with the ability to manipulate themselves into animals and possibly control them, dependent on their abilities. Our magic..." He paused, a bright silver coursed over his body as he called a wolf to his side, emerging from the wall behind him. "...is branded in silver." The Chancellor looked down at the wolf who whined and stood at attention next to his leg, ready to pounce should she need to.

"So... why me? I don't... I'm not some witch or something. I'm a bartender for Christ's sake. Sure we have a similar little birthmark but other than that, I got nothing," Cassidy said, glancing around. That was when Chase perked up.

"And that's where you're wrong," he said, his voice as strong as ever as he stood up in front of her. "The night of your accident, we were tracking the leeches. They only ever surface when they have found something worth risking their lives for and, it didn't take me long to stumble upon you. When your signet triggered, it sent out a pulse to anyone within range. It's how I knew where you were. It's how I got to you just in the knick of time. That mark saved you," Chase said. He wasn't going to play loose with the truth. If she was going to be one of them, she needed to know what was going on.

"Alright, say I believe you. Say I believe this isn't just some weird concussion nightmare I'm having because I thought the guy who saved me was hot," she said, rolling her eyes when Chase's smirk grew. "What the hell are leeches? Why were they wanting me?"

The Chancellor perked up at her question, taking the reigns of the conversation once more. "Leeches is a derogatory term. There are members of our group that are no longer with us. While we tolerate almost any kind of behavior, knowing that magical or not, issues arise, there are a few rules we will not allow to be broken. No member of the Exodus shall kill another member or expose themselves to a human. The biggest rule is no one can forcibly trigger a signet. The beauty of the evolution of our bodies is that the trigger should be honest and untouched. Forcing someone to trigger before they are ready or before they have been deemed able by the powers above is the biggest law we have. If you break said laws, you will be expelled from our community. No help, no communication, everything severed. We are very much a family and your Origin, wherever you find yourself, will become like a part of you. And to break yourself off from the Exodus is nearly like giving up a part of yourself. So, the members that have been excommunicated banded together, to try and tear us down. They named themselves the League but most Exodus members call them Leeches because they go out and find recently triggered signets and try to suck away their abilities or recruit them for themselves. It really is a dangerous and deplorable group of people." The Chancellor's disdain grew tenfold as he spoke of the League. The hatred was nearly palpable as he spoke but his demeanor changed when he glanced back at Cassidy with a smile.

"But, none of that matters because you're here, where you're supposed to be. And we will keep you safe, teach you how to become a powerful Origin wielder. And Chase will be your help along the way, even if you're in separate origins," he said, beckoning to Chase who moved closer to Cassidy.

"Why him?" she said, arching a brow at the man and then glancing to the Chancellor.

"Because, you and he are joined," he said simply and the confusion on Cassidy's face made him chuckle.

"I'm sorry, I forget how many people don't know our cultures. Being joined isn't a rarity but it isn't terribly common either. Since forcibly triggering someone is illegal, when it happens, a bond is made, and it's the reason it's illegal in the first place. When a member brings someone back to life, in the event of them becoming triggered themselves, they become joined. You two will be stronger together. You'll learn his ins and outs, possibly predict movements, be dependent upon one another in a fight or even just every day. It's a bond that connects your souls and connects to your magic as well. It is something that the two of you will work on once an Origin picks you," he said, Cassidy's cheeks turning flush as he explained what joining is. She did perk up at the end of the conversation, when he mentioned when the Origin picks her.

"There's another thing I don't get to pick?" she asked with a slight of anger. She didn't appreciate being linked to someone whom she didn't know or even possibly like. The Chancellor smiled and went behind his desk, flipping through his pages before his eyes rested on her.

"Much like everything else in magic, it picks you. Your soul will call to one of the origins. And, that will be your home."

Chapter 5

Chase had escorted them from the Chancellor's office and out to a rather luxurious foyer, Cassidy chewing on her bottom lip as her arms crossed over her chest, hugging her tightly.

"You're nervous," he said, more as a statement than a question and she was so enthralled at something on the floor that she didn't even hear what he had said.

"Huh?" she asked, snapping her head up to look at him and shaking her head, her shoulders dropping low as she tried to process everything the Chancellor told her over the past hour.

"I said, you seem nervous. Your energy, you alright?" he asked, arching a brow and she shifted her weight uncomfortably.

"Don't do that," she said, her voice slightly cold as she leaned back against the ornate wall, running her hand over her face and breathing as calmly as she could. "Don't do your... mind or bond shit on me, okay. I never asked for any of this. I never asked for you. I definitely didn't ask for you to save me so don't go reading me," she snapped.

Chase's eyes narrowed quickly, shaking his head before he spoke. "You didn't ask for me to save you but I did and I was there and now there's a bond between us that you'll get to have for the rest of your life. We're a part of you now. I'm a part of you now. So, like it or not, I'm not going anywhere and maybe you'll learn to understand why I did what I did in the first place with time. I wasn't going to just let you die." Chase didn't like the tone she decided to take with him, especially with everything that she had just learned. "And, before you think that you're some special gift, I didn't have to use my Origin to tell that you were nervous. Your flushed, your hugging your arms to your chest, sorry I'm perceptive," he finished.

Cassidy ran her tongue over the bottom of her lip, angry at him, angry at the situation and angry at herself. It was a situation that didn't appear to be getting any better as she continued on and she was taking it out on everyone else instead of dealing with it.

"How can you expect to tell someone this after everything that's happened to me and expect me to be okay right now?" Her voice sounded like it was going to break and Chase walked over to her, stepping to stand in front of her and her hands dropped to her sides, trying to put on a strong face.

"Because, we've all been in your shoes before," he said softly, reminding her that the path to triggering a signet all ended the same way. Death. She bit her bottom lip, closed her eyes and nodded, hating herself just a bit more for sounding so whiny in a situation in which he had faced himself whenever he was triggered.

"I know it's been a lot but, you've got about an hour or so until they round up the other signets triggered in the past few days for Origin selection. You should probably head down to the grand ballroom and mingle for a bit. I'll be down there once it all starts but I need to finish some things with the Chancellor beforehand. You think you can find your way well enough?" Chase took a step back away from her as he watched her, trying his best to stay out her head while she thought through his question.

"Yeah, yeah, I think, yeah, I've got it." She nodded, pushing herself off of the wall and running her fingers through the hem of her tank top, pulling it down and taking a step towards the hall in front of her that lead her to the rest of the building. Chase looked her over one last time before nodding, heading back towards the Chancellor's office and leaving Cassidy alone for the first time since they arrived.

"Yeah, I can do this," she muttered, glancing back towards the office before continuing the long walk down the corridor. There were a few photos, some symbols that she didn't recognize but other than that, it really seemed somewhat lifeless. It wasn't a school, she could understand that much. It was more... a collection of people than anything else. Chase was obviously in his mid twenties, the Chancellor well over sixty and herself being twenty-two, there was no way she was going back to school. Not even magic school.

Her fingers brushed the wall as she rounded the corner, listening as the sounds further down towards the ballroom grew. Someone pushed open one of the doors, the sounds of a full on party pulsing down the corridor and Cassidy grinned slightly. Through the whirlwind of emotions, a party was something she could get behind. One last step and one last breath and before she knew it, she was pulled into the grand ballroom.

The room had a pulse that was indescribable. The beat through the room filled her chest and her heart started to race. The colors of the origins moved across the room as five pedelstals sat in the dead center of the room. Each had it's greek symbol emblazoned in granite, the designation of the five origins the Chancellor had gone over earlier in the day.

There was probably over two hundred people packed into the room, laughing and talking amongst themselves. The ages ranged from preteen to all the way up to the elderly few off to the edges. It was such a strange place to be in but it was like she was made to be in that room. She actually felt like she was at home.

"Oi! Why don't you have a drink? All newbies have to have a drink!" A voice rang out, handing Cassidy the glowing yellow drink and laughing. The woman had fiery red hair and more noticeable than that was the sprawling tattoo that started below her shoulder and crawled up her neck, taking over her entire right side. It was intricately designed, a Mendala sort of style that made the drawing look like lace up her side. However distracting it was, it was insanely beautiful.

"Katherine," she said, pointing to herself with a grin, taking a hefty drink before sparking the blue over her hands to denote her Origin. "Omicron, if you were curious. You're Chase's find, yeah?" she questioned and Cassidy nodded as she found her lips to the straw of the drink and took a sip. The drink instantly warmed her from the inside, opening up her senses and making the feel of her heartbeat more sensitive than it was earlier.

"Whoa," she laughed, glancing at the drink while Katherine grinned.

"Dosed booze. Great in moderation but can take you for a hell of a ride the first time out. Be careful!" she said, squeezing her hand before letting her go and continuing on with the party.

A few more minutes passed, Cassidy making small talk with a few from Sigma, the Necromancy Origin. She anticipated that many of them would be very standoffish but it seemed that everyone in the room was rather welcoming. She couldn't peg if it was because any of them could share an Origin or not but it was nice to be apart of a room so full of life—especially with so many able to control life and death.

After speaking with a few more people, the Chancellor

made his way into the chamber, grasping the hands of a few along the path to the pedestals that were ready to be greeted by the newest of active signets.

"Settle down, settle down. I know, everyone is very excited to see how the events of the night go but, patience. It's a virtue I know most of you don't have," he said with a grin, causing a few of the already initiated members to laugh before addressing the new people to the room. "There are fourteen of you here today to find which Origin you belong in. This is a ceremony that we've all been through and one that is a long time coming for all of you. Your signet was there since birth. This Origin has always been a part of you and now, the world will know where your soul belongs. Taking on the connection to an Origin is a process no one should take lightly. By stepping forward and committing to an Origin, you pledge to protect and uphold the laws that the Exodus have created for centuries. You will strive to learn more and teach along the way and to always hold the respect of your Origin along with others above everything else." The Chancellor spoke in a tone that was rather soothing and it wasn't long before Cassidy was drinking the koolaide. The entire ceremony process was foreign to her but she was more than excited to embark on an adventure that gave her a family and a purpose. Especially after the past year.

The first four people went, coming to the pedestals and touching each symbol on the granite before finding which they belonged to. The granite would glow the color of its respective branded magic and the other four pedestals would disappear. The first two people went to Omicron, the healing Origin. The next to Sigma, the necromancy Origin, Chi after that, the telekinetic Origin and before Cassidy knew it, it was her turn.

Her name echoed through the hall, a few mumbles about who she was spreading across the room. Being joined wasn't a common occurrence and it was quickly spread around that she was one of the newest triggered signets ready to find her

36 Epsilon

Origin. The fact that she was joined to another Chi made it highly likely that she too, would be a Chi. Cassidy didn't really know where she belonged.

Her steps carried her into the center of the pedestals and it wasn't long before she was seeking out someone in front of her that she recognized. She was thankful that she wasn't going first, at least. The Chancellor urged her to push forward, Cassidy lifting her gaze amongst the crowd, everyone waiting on baited breath for her to find where she would end up.

Just breathe, Cassidy. One of them is your home. You'll find it.

Her head snapped up to find Chase when she heard his voice in her head, almost ready to respond to him aloud until she realized that he was in her head. It took her a moment to spot his tousled hair in the back of the room but it didn't take him more than a second to show a cocky grin that was practically permanently etched on his face.

Cassidy laughed softly, glancing away from him before looking at the pedestals. With a deep breath, she moved forward to the Chi symbol, assuming, like everyone else, that was where she was destined to go. And, about a moment after her hand rested on the granite, the pedestal sunk away from her and disappeared within the floor.

There were a few gasps when the Chi symbol didn't react to her hand and Cassidy quickly glance up to Chase to confirm she should continue. He gave her a nod and the Chancellor followed suit as she moved on to the Delta symbol, her hand grazing the stone and it shuddered away from her touch, sinking into the ground faster than the Chi element had. Cassidy decided that she wanted to just continue to go through the circle until one reacted to her and right as she was about to touch the Omicron symbol, she turned and faced the Epsilon one. A quick intake of breath and before she could direct herself to walk towards it, her feet were already moving. It was as if there was a pull, unbeknownst to her, that she needed to go and touch that pedestal.

Cassidy's hand connected with the pillar and unlike the others, the Epsilon pillar pulsed a bright and vibrant green color, enveloping around her hand and then around her body as the rest of the pillars sunk to the ground. A heavy breeze rocked through the room as the other Epsilons around her showed off their green energy, calling forth all the elements at once to make the overwhelming feeling that much stronger. Touching the pedestal was like completing a part of her body. All the anticipation rolled off in waves, a calm she had never experienced before taking its place. It was as if a gaping hole in her soul was filled. Complete, even.

For the first time in her life, she felt truly and completely at home.

"Cassidy Hawkins, welcome to Epsilon," the Chancellor spoke, all the Epsilon members sparking the green into the air as the magic settled into her hands. Cassidy lifted her hand, staring at her palm and then to her arms, watching as the green light ebbed and flowed from her skin.

Within the group, an older woman, in her mid forties, came through the crowd to greet Cassidy.

"I'm Rebecca, Elder of Epsilon. Welcome home," she said, the smile gracing her features. Her hair was a dirty blonde with a few strands of gray, her signet was on the inside of her right wrist, easily seen as she stood in front of Cassidy. Once the elder said welcome home, the rest of Epsilon uttered welcome home with a few cheers and excited exclamations in the back. Cassidy laughed, glancing around as all the eyes were on her and she held a ball of green energy in her hands before clasping them closed. It was a feeling she'd never experienced before. And, she was loving it.

Chapter 6

When the Chancellor said that the Exodus would become her family, he wasn't kidding. The minute the Epsilon pedestal ignited green, Cassidy was given all the rights and privileges of an Exodus member. A room was perhaps her biggest highlight. Rebecca gave her the keys to her home away from home after the ceremony ended. It took her a little while to navigate through the halls and rooms, trying desperately to find where her room was within the compound. Hell, at this point, she didn't even know where she was in relation to her home. Everything was happening so fast and Cassidy was trying to absorb everything as it came at her.

Finally finding the hall in which her room was connected, she walked down until the fourth door on the right, seeing her name engraved into the gold plate to the right of the door. "Cool," she muttered, slipping the key into the slot and knocking as she opened the door. Inside was one large king bed, adorned with lavish sheets and bedding. There was a desk with a few books—basic elemental magic being one of them—and a small lamp. The room led into a kitchenette and then into a rather large ensuite bathroom with a tile tub and vanity mirror set. It was as if the room was like a hotel and it was lovely. It almost made her forget about everything that happened over the past few weeks. Almost.

On the table was a letter addressed to her, written in Rebecca's handwriting. Her name was delicately sprawled across the top and it made her heart skip a beat. Another surprise?

> I hope all the accommodations are to your liking. If you need anything, simply ask Geoff. He's our housing liasion for Epsilon and he'll make sure you're taken care of. You've been paired up with Olivia as your mentor within Epsilon. She'll help guide you within the Origin, help you with your magic, teach you the basics. Chase will be around for things but Olivia is a member of our Origin and greatly respected within our circles. I'm sure you'll love her. If you need me, you'll know how to contact me soon enough. —R

Cassidy left the note on the table, plopping down on the bed, kicking off her shoes and laying down, staring at the ceiling. My, how her life had changed.

A few minutes passed as she simply sat in silence, letting the beat of her heart lull her into a calm before she lifted her hands to stare at them. She thought, at first, that just thinking about her Origin would bring it to the surface, expecting the green to wrap itself around her skin and ignite the room. But, it was obvious that wasn't the case.

At twenty minutes into trying to will her magic to the surface, a knock echoed on the wood of her door which snapped her head up towards the noise. Answering it, there was a very petite woman, late teens or early twenties with bright green eyes and black hair.

"You must be Olivia?" Cassidy asked, arching a brow at the woman and managing a gentle smile, Olivia returning the gesture in kind.

"That'd be me. If Rebecca didn't tell me that she told you I'd be by, I'd think you really were meant to be in Chi," she said with a laugh, leaning into the nook of the door. "So, ready to get down to the nitty gritty? Not saying the Origin ceremony isn't fun but... learning the Origin is far more entertaining. And thrilling," she said, her grin growing as did Cassidy's.

"This is gonna get me in trouble," Cassidy muttered, glancing back to her room for a minute before flipping the lock on the handle, closing the door behind her and slipping the key in her back pocket, ready for what Olivia wanted to show her. "Lead the way," she said, ushering her arm in front of her.

Olivia nodded, grabbing her phone from her back pockets and sending off a quick text before stashing it away again, looking up to Cassidy and clapping her hands together. "So, you've got to have questions. What do you want to start off with first?" she asked, walking down the corridor at the same pace as Cassidy.

"How do I make it work?" she blurted out, a slight tinge of pink igniting her cheeks before looking to her hands. "I mean, I've been trying for about the past half hour and it's really starting to piss me off," she laughed. Olivia nodded, lifting her hand up and igniting the green instantly, a quick breeze passing past them in the hall.

"See! That! How'd you do that?" Cassidy exclaimed, staring at her hands in anger.

"Well, first, origins are grounded in not only your emotions but also your soul. It was a gift that was bestowed upon us at birth. And, something that's brewed inside you for the past twenty-two years, just begging to break the surface. Now that it has, it's not used to the freedom. So, you have to learn to channel it," she said, stopping the walk down the hall and facing Cassidy, grabbing her hands in the process. "Here. Close your eyes," she said, Cassidy looking down the hall before looking back to Olivia and closing her eyes. "Now, take a deep breath. Hold it in for a few seconds, maybe even a second longer than you think you can and then blow it out, slowly," she instructed, watching as Cassidy followed her to a T. "Now, clear your mind. You're an Epsilon. Your magic, more than anyone else, starts at your core. Your body is a vessel. Now, take that power, that surge of energy that you never really noticied before until now, and channel it. Think about what you want, what you need, and make it a reality." Olivia's voice was soothing, almost entrancing as Cassidy listened. Each word drew her in deeper and deeper and before she knew it, the warmth spread across her hands. Her breath caught in her throat, her eyes opening only when she knew she'd conjured it to her hands and the wind whipped around them instantly. The wind grew rather quickly, both Cassidy and Olivia's hair an uncontrollable mess as Olivia grabbed her hands, bringing Cassidy back to the moment, the wind stopping almost immediately.

"Control is something you'll learn in time. There are several elements that you have the ability to tap into now. And each have a different... taste to them," she grinned, snapping her fingers and calling a flame to her hand, the green magic glowing with the red of the flame. "Each element will conjure a different feeling within you. You'll generally have one that you'll specialize in more than others but no one will know until you do," she shrugged.

Cassidy turned to continue down the hall, fiddling with her fingernails as they walked once more. "So, when Chase came to my house, to tell me about, well, all of this," she laughed, shaking her head as she thought back to earlier in the day, "he insisted that he needed an invitation to come inside, even though we were being attacked by some psycho gree..." She trailed off, clasping her hand over her face as she looked up to

Olivia. "I-I'm sorry. I didn't mean... she just attacked me so—" she said, glancing back to the halls in front of them as they walked. It didn't click in her head that when she became a member of Epsilon, she was apart of the same Origin that Geneva once belonged to. Olivia would know her.

"Don't apologize. She made her bed, now she has to lie in it." Olivia shrugged, trying not to seem upset by the fact that Geneva was no longer with Exodus. "And, in regards to the invitation, it goes back to how we become triggered. Technically we died. But, now that we're alive and kicking once again, the signet is active. It's not required with everyone but, if you go to a triggered signets home, you'll have to get an invitation to come in. It's kind of... the signets way of protecting you. Not everyone is so nice. Or welcoming." Olivia's word had a tinge of a warning to them but they mostly were just truth, a truth proven by Geneva's attack on her home already.

"Guess that makes sense," she said, glancing to where her signet was, knowing that she couldn't see it with her shoes on but that the simply mark was now changing her life tenfold. "How long have you been triggered?" Cassidy asked, rounding the corner towards one of the larger buildings in the complex.

"I was seven." She nodded, opening one of the doors and rounding the corner to a room practically a shrine of sorts to Epsilon. Photos, symbols, green tinges all around. The room itself felt warm and inviting and she was instantly settled being inside. Olivia laughed when she noticed Cassidy's body react to the room. "It's seeped in our Origin magic. You'll heal faster in here, react quicker, think clearer and feel centered. It's a channelling room," she said, pulling out a chair along with Cassidy.

"Right, because, that's something I'll need now," she laughed, looking over the room towards a few others that were sitting and chatting, two off in the distance sitting with the green pulse circling around them. "But, seven? Holy shit," she said, snapping back to their conversation. Olivia shrugged, fiddling with her phone once more before looking back to Cassidy. "I was shot in a robbery. My mom and me. She was fine but it nicked an artery on me and my heart stopped for twenty-three seconds. Docs managed to patch me up, mainly because one was Omicron and we didn't even know it," she laughed. The luck this woman had was impeccable. Cassidy pulled her feet underneath her in her seat, leaning over the chair arm as she took in the story. Learning all of this at seven? That had to have been a challenge, far more than at twenty-two.

"But, it brought me all of this. Now that you're here, you'll feel it too. It feels right. Like, I never knew I was missing a big part of me before now but ever since coming here and experiencing all of this, I realize I'm one of the lucky ones. Some go untriggered for life. I only missed out for seven years," she said, matter of factly. Olivia was right, though, and Cassidy could feel it. Every fiber of her being started to crave the abilities swimming beneath her skin. One might even say it's addicting.

"Showing her the ropes already?" a voice asked, a man by the name of Killian who towered over many of the other people in the room, long, shoulder length hair and deep brown eyes, came over to the two girls who were seated. Olivia nodded, gesturing towards the newly arrived guest.

"This is Killian, his specialty is electricity," she said, Killian producing the vibrant green energy to his fingers, a quick spark joining in. Cassidy arched a brow at the element before nodding a hello in his direction.

"So, we don't just cover wind, fire, water and earth?" she questioned, leaning in ever so intently to listen. Olivia laughed, shaking her head.

"We're an Origin grounded in the elements. Any element. Fire, water, air, ice, earth, electric, metal, wood... I could name off our abilities one by one until I got blue in the face. And, there are probably some that I'll forget or don't even know about along the way. This Origin surprises me daily," she smiled, Killian nodding as she spoke.

"Which is why you can only do magic from your Origin." Killian spoke up, glancing around him before looking back to Cassidy. "Epsilon chose us. So, elemental magic is all we can do. There's never been a known case of someone triggered being able to use more than one Origin, at least... not yet," he said, wiggling his eyebrows with a laugh before relaxing back against the couch.

"What do you mean?" Cassidy questioned, looking to Olivia for clarification. Olivia rolled her eyes at Killian's suggestion before answering Cassidy.

"Supposedly, a bunch of Chis back... who knows how long ago, predicted that there would be one who could wield all five origins at once," she said, nonchalantly, almost as if she didn't believe it. Killian quickly snapped his tongue against his teeth in a tsking noise, cutting her off.

"Don't listen to her, she isn't a believer," Killian said teasingly, running his hand through his hair, some thread bracelets on his wrist showing underneath his long sleeves.

"No, I just don't think that prophecies or predicting the future in our world is not necessarily something to bank on. You see what we can do, what we all can do. Who's to say a centuries old prophecy or sight is still valid? What if the person who was supposed to be the one never got triggered? Too many variables," Olivia reasoned, valid thoughts on all accounts.

"Nah, see, you can't think like that. Supposedly the prophecy was foretold by the original Chancellor. So, say what you want but I gotta believe in one of the most powerful Chis this world has ever seen. And you didn't even mention the best part." He grinned, looking back to Cassidy, acting like he was telling a ghost story. "The prophecy states that the person who wields the five origins will either unite the five origins and usher in a period of greatness or destroy the origins and bring great ruin," he said, a roll of thunder taking over the room as he finished, Olivia laughing at his dramatics and Cassidy jumped when the thunder started. Killian laughed, running his hand over his chin as he subsided the thunder he rolled in, putting his hands up in apologies. "Sorry, too good to pass up."

Cassidy narrowed her eyes for a minute at his apology before glancing around the room, all the eyes on her. She felt the flush to her cheeks increase, sinking back into her chair before looking to Olivia. It never even crossed her mind that there would be people who could predict the future or prophesize.

"Don't worry. Most of us don't even recognize things said with the sight. Some hold it as law and then some regard it as just crazy dreams. Besides, no one has ever been able to hold two origins, let alone all five. And, if someone could, we'd know about it by now," Olivia reassured her, heading to the small fridge by the bookcase and grabbing herself a water before sitting back down.

Cassidy nodded at Olivia's remark, calming herself at the thought of something possibly taking this all away from her. It might have only been a day so far but she felt more connected in a day than she had for the twenty-two previous years before it all. And that wasn't something she planned on losing, ever.

"What's your specialty?" Cassidy asked of Olivia after a few moments passed, Olivia finishing up her sip of water before shaking the bottle.

"Water." She grinned, taking a bit of the water from the bottle and holding it in her palm, creating a tiny water tornado in her hand. Cassidy watched as the water twirled, Olivia making a tiny strike of lighting in her palm as clouds moved over it, an entire scene of a storm playing out in her hand.

"Now that, is cool." Cassidy grinned, looking to her hands and breathing a bit slower, concentrating on pulling an element up through her magic, even if just for a minute. She stared at her hand, concentrating and becoming frustrated that nothing was coming to the surface. To say she was impatient was an understatement. Right as she decided to quit, a bright red flame ignited across her hand, the green swell of magic protecting it from harm as she gasped. She held it closer to her face, the fire spreading up her forearm before she shook it away.

"Fire is easy when you're angry. Water is easy when you're calm. Earth comes easy to those who nurture or love. Air develops from patience. It really just depends on your mood," Killian said, nodding towards other Epsilons in the area. "Like Derrick, he has an affinity for earth. Abigail is wicked good at air. And Wesley is the best fire wielder I know," he finished, pointing them out as he spoke. Derrick was a dark skinned man, in his late twenties. He was shorter than Killian but not by much and appeared to be married to Abigail. Abigail was a medium built woman with brown hair and glasses but, even from a distance, it was clear that she put off a motherly nature. And Wesley was probably the eldest in the room, in his late forties with a full salt and pepper beard and brown with flecks of gray hair, along with hazel eyes.

Cassidy took in the information and pseudo introductions as best she could, listening to them both go on and on about how to wield her magic efficiently, how to use it, how to control it under areas of pressure, etc. It was a wealth of knowledge to learn but also overwhelming.

"You know what, I think I'm done for the day." She laughed, capping her water bottle she'd got after sitting in the room for several hours, notebooks and pens strewn out in front of the three of them. Cassidy appreciated all the notes and drawings, even making light of their situation several times and she definitely felt the bonds of friendship forming just from the few hours of conversation. It was nice to have someone to listen to her for once, especially with them both having gone through the same thing along with sharing an Origin together.

Olivia nodded, tying her hair up in a bun before glancing to Killian. "Yeah, we should probably head up too," she said, resting her hand on Killian's knee and the man running his hand over hers. The entire conversation made far more sense now that she could see that they were together. Their energy was nearly palpable.

Cassidy stood, running her hands over her thighs as Killian asked if she needed help. "I think I got it. And, if I get lost? Gotta figure my way out sometime." She grinned, tossing her bottle in the recycle bin near the door. "Thanks, for everything," she said, giving them a smile as they nodded back.

"Anytime," Killian said, giving her a wave. "We'll see ya around." Cassidy laughed once more before spinning on her heel and heading out into the hallway.

Instantly walking out of the room made her feel a sudden surge of energy wane from her. She'd forgotten how the room was an Epsilon channeling area and created in Origin magic. It powered her more than she could tell and it wasn't long before she realized how tired she actually was.

"finding your Origin takes a lot out of you," Chase called, rounding the corner to come up beside her, glancing down at her face when she looked up to him. Chase looked just as tired as she was, wearing a zip up hoodie over the clothes he had on earlier. His blue eyes looked into hers, Cassidy feeling the pull that others had spoken about earlier due to the fact that they were joined. It wasn't so much as a need to be around one another but it was obvious when he was standing next to her that her soul pulled to his. Cassidy was unsure of how she felt about it, if she were honest. Everything about the Exodus was amazing. Except for the fact that she was now forever bound to him. It wasn't that he was a bad person... or even bad to look at, she just didn't like that her soul pulled to someone so involuntarily. She didn't know him. She barely knew his name, let alone anything particularly about him. Age, middle name, favorite food. These were things that she thought were fairly important given their proximity to each other.

"Yeah, you find yours today too?" she asked with a grin, arching a brow at him which got a chuckle.

"Cute," he said, shaking his head with a shrug. "Been a long day for me too. Had to save your ass, remember? Plus, we're linked. You get drained, it wanes on me too," he reminded. Cassidy frowned, nodding her head.

"Lots of things I have to get used to. Generally I'm only worried about myself and usually, I'm not too concerned in that aspect." Chase thought on her statement for a second, guiding her turns down towards her room when she nearly went the wrong way.

"Well, you're part of something bigger now. Not only are we connected but when you placed your hand on that pillar, you connected with everyone else in Epsilon. You hurt the Origin if you get too roughed up. Everyone would know if you died," he said, gazing down at her. "I'm not saying they'd know anything else but if you drained out your magic or were mortally injured, they'd have a feeling. And, so would I." Chase didn't know how great he felt about being connected to someone either. He didn't feel comfortable with vulnerability. It was a new feeling for him and one he would never get used to.

"Yeah yeah, I get it. Everything is bigger than me now. Check in that box, complete," she said with a yawn, recognizing her hall as they walked down towards her new room. "I'll get to go... live a normal life still, right? I mean, I have bills to pay, friends who care about me, a house to live in... this... all of this is wonderful. And exciting. I just want to make sure I can stay me," she said, fumbling for her keys.

"But you're not you anymore. You're better than old you," he said bluntly. "But, yes. Your home is still there. If you decided to go back, it'd probably be soon after you felt comfortable in a fight. Geneva and the leeches won't let you be for long. They'll either try and get you to come to their side or drain you of your magic. Currently, you're in no position to fight them with any expectancy of winning," Chase said, following in after her, Cassidy closing the door behind them.

"Then let's go. Teach me, I'm ready," she said, standing in front of him, hands summoned green as the magic coursed across her skin, Chase shaking his head. It was apparent that she was exhausted. The circle under her eyes, the more pale than vibrant green color ebbing from her hands, she needed rest, not training.

"Yes, energizer bunny. Another night. One where you can stand up without falling over, yeah?" he said, glancing around her room and then back to her. "I'll see you in the morning," he said with a nod, teleported to his place before she could even say bye.

"We're gonna have to work on that!" she called out, assuming he could hear her.

Chapter 7

Ugh," Cassidy grunted, her face slamming against the ground as the red pulsed brightly around her body, quickly dissipating once she connected with the ground. Chase was roughly thirty yards away from her, pacing back and forth in a pair of dark wash jeans, a black crew neck shirt, his stereotypical chuck taylors and a bit of sweat rolling from his brow. They'd been going back and forth at it for nearly an hour now, training and pushing Cassidy's abilities to make her a substantial fighter. A weapon, even.

"Come on, Cass. You're not even trying anymore," he scolded, Cassidy groaning as she rolled off of the floor, wearing a pair of shorts and a black tank top, a gray and pink sports bra underneath and her hair pulled up into a bun.

"You're beginning to piss me off," she said, fists clenched closed as she brushed away the sweat from her brow. Chase scoffed, pacing back and forth for a moment before firing a bolt of red dead in her chest, Cassidy caught off guard that he'd attack her so quickly after just getting back up. She slammed against the back wall, the breath escaping her chest and her ears ringing from the impact. Her body crumpled to the ground, hand moving to her head as it sounded like she was whimpering in pain. Chase felt the deep surge of pain radiate through their bond and moved go help her to her feet. Maybe he pushed her too hard this time.

"Hey," he said, about ten feet from her, lending his hand out to help her to her feet and once he was within distance, the green energy expelled from her core, down her arms and through her fingers, a quick burst of air picking him up near the roof and then promptly slamming him against the floor with a deafening thud. Cassidy clamored to her feet, a small line of blood trailing under her nose as she exhausted a large chunk of energy.

"Don't ever underestimate your opponent," she said weakly with a fake bravado as she repeated his verbage from their first session. The same surge that Chase had felt from Cassidy's injuries, she now was feeling from his, glancing to where his body was on the ground but when she looked to the spot, he was no longer there. Within a fraction of a second, her arms wrapped behind her body, his grip on her arms light a straight jacket as she tried to rip herself free.

"The statement still stands," he said with a grunt as she struggled, Cassidy digging her nails into his hands but not causing him to loosen his grip at all. As she tried to free herself, her hands became increasingly warm, channeling the fire element through her skin until Chase thought the pain was unbearable and released her, pushing her out and away from him as he shook the heat from his hands.

"Alright, alright," he said, putting his hands up in the air as he looked her over. Between the sweat and the blood, it looked like they'd been going on hours of sparring and training but at least she was getting better. What she lacked in strength, she made up for in smarts. You didn't always need to be more powerful than your opponent but being smarter nearly always got you to win.

"Hey, I tried to quit an hour ago but you had to keep pushing," she groaned, glancing in the large mirror that allowed them to watch their form as they moved in the sparring room. Below the sports bra was a bright raw bruise that had grown within the course of about twenty minutes. It seemed that she probably had cracked a rib but until she saw an Omicron to confirm, she'd have no idea.

Chase felt slightly guilty about the harm he'd caused her. On one hand there was the part of him that felt a distaste for letting anyone—women or men—get harmed at his hand but the other aspect was the fact that he was keeping her from dying. The bruises, the blood, the exhaustion, it all had a purpose. Anyone before a war would train their best fighters to become even better and that was what he was going to do.

"You can schedule a minute with Omicron in the morning. They'll probably be able to get you in first thing," he said, grabbing up his water bottle and downing a good portion of it before watching Cassidy did the same.

"Nah, I'm alright. Nothing that's going to kill me so, I can heal myself," she said, snatching up a towel to the left of her bottle and wiping it out from under her nose. It'd become a rather normal reaction as to when she used more magic than her body could handle.

"You know, this whole Origin thing, we have the ability to skip the shitty downtime aspect of the human body. Evolution or fate or whatever you think brought you here, brought you here knowing that you could go to someone and within ten seconds, be healed up, good as new. At least if you were an Omicron, I wouldn't have to push you as much as I do," he said, the frustration building as he tried to swallow it back, shoving the towel and water bottle in his bag as he waited for her retort. Because, if there was one thing Cassidy Hawkins was great about, it was ensuring she had the last word in an argument.

"No one went and asked you to train me. Or try and

protect me. Or push me. You might not be used to it but… I can take care of myself just fine. I don't need you to be here. You want to be here and while I get that, don't pin your worry and want to control every little thing of your life on me. That's your own problem to deal with. If you can't take letting me train the way I want to, I'll just go back to letting Olivia guide me. It's what she's meant to do anyway." Cassidy at least was fiercely independent in most aspects of her life.

"I don't mind being in here and training with you. That's part of the luxury of being joined to you but you also don't need to be making yourself weak on purpose! All I'm asking is that you take fifteen minutes and see someone to get healed up so you're ready to go at a moment's notice. That's all. You're being unreasonable." Chase pointed at her as he slipped the bag over his shoulders, his hands resting on the straps.

"Pain is a real element to life. It reminds us that we're human. It causes us to focus more on the subject at hand. It prepares us for a real life situation. I might get my ass handed to myself one day and then be up shit creek because an Omicron isn't there to help. So, I might be in a position where I'm injured and I have to deal with that. If I were mortally wounded, of fucking course I'd be in there right now asking for help… but not like this. It's my ribs. I'm not having troubles breathing. I'll be fine." Cassidy's biggest struggle since becoming an Exodus member was remembering that she was human. She'd been in the compound for weeks now after her ceremony, not even leaving the compound to go home. It was voluntary, of course. She could go home at any time, she just chose not to and it was constantly recommended not to. Between Geneva and the League and her rather strong abilities that she wasn't too sure she'd be able to keep in check around humans, it was safer this way. But, all the secrecy was causing her to become restless.

"Well aren't you just a bunch of sunshine and roses," he teased, waiting for her to get her bags put together. They'd been training every day for the past five weeks and each day, they learned more and more about each other. But, it was apparent that the constant training was waning on Cassidy's good nature.

"Maybe you should go back home or work, for a day or so. Or, however you'd like," he offered as they walked out of the room and back towards her living quarters. Cassidy arched a brow questioningly at him, licking her lips.

"But, I thought it wasn't safe for me to be there? You said—"

"I know what I've said about it," he said, cutting her off. "But, I also think letting you go and work or be a bit normal for a day would be good for you. You know how to defend yourself if need be and all you have to do is think about me and I'll be there, if you need me," he reminded her, stopping and brushing a stray hair behind her ear. Cassidy looked up at him and swallowed hard, chewing on the inside of her bottom lip.

"Yeah, yeah, I could go to work," she said, nodding her head. "But how do I explain why I've been gone?" Cassidy hadn't came in for a shift for weeks now. The only time they left was to get Ruca and her things and that was shortly after she became an Epsilon.

"I've already taken care of that," Chase laughed, tapping his temple with a glowing red finger. "He approved some emotional time for you and told me whenever you wanted to come back that he'd be lucky to have you," Chase said with a grin, feeling the rush of excitement stemming from Cassidy at the thought of returning back to work. "Go, I know you want to. I'll come find you if I need you," he said, turning away from her and heading towards his room within the compound.

"Thank you," she said with his back to her. "We seriously need to work on you finishing a conversation before just walking off!" She yelled, him putting his hand in the air and waving her off. Cassidy rolled her eyes and walked back to her room without another word.

56 Epsilon

She peeled her work out clothes off, starting up the shower in her bathroom as the steam started to fog up the mirror in front of her. A quick wave of her hand and glow of green pushed the steam into the shower only and she avoided the small mishap of being unable to see herself. There were several bruises that peppered her skin, a few in the yellow/green stage and several still in the red/purple arena. Long days and nights pushing herself, pushing her abilities and pushing her knowledge had culminated in her being one of the fastest trained Epsilons that the Exodus had seen in years. Currently fire was her element of choice, rising up easily with her heated temper but the others were just as entertaining for her. If anything, trying them all seemed to thrill her more than anything. And, being the best she could possibly be.

She reached up and wiped away the smidge of blood that she had missed when she cleaned up her face earlier, stepping into the shower, a groan slipping from her lips at the scorching water hit her skin. Her muscles took the pain and welcomed it, the heat helping them relax as she tried to settle after such a long training session. Based on the time of the day, she could easily get out to Charlie's and serve a shift before the night was up. It probably wasn't as soon as Chase would've hoped but the man had a point. Cassidy was still worried that she would lose herself to the magic and knowledge of the Exodus life. And while some found everything they needed within the compound walls, Cassidy still held out an opinion on that thought. Could she continue to live solely within and around Exodus members? Could she mingle out within the rest of the world and not think less of them?

Clearly, it was time to find out.

Cassidy finished up her shower, straightening the curl out of her hair and it coming to right above her ribcage. Eyelids framed with bright gold eyeshadow and winged liner, fiercely curled eyelashes simply highlighted her blue eyes more than normal. Her shirt was a vneck, Charlie's etched across her chest in a logo style and this time paired with dark wash jeans and a pair of calf boots. Normally, she'd go for the outfits that would get her a decent sized tip while bartending but while her body, under her clothes, looked as if she were run over by a large car, she didn't want to field questions she didn't have appropriate answers for. At least, not yet. She sent a quick message to let Olivia know that she was going to work and thought about Chase before their joined link came up in her head.

Taking your advice, heading to Charlie's. Promise I'll be safe.

Good. Enjoy. Be safe.

Relax. If I can kick your ass, I can kick anyone's.

Cassidy disconnected their connection soon after she told him her last thought, grabbing up her bags and heading to the main gate of the Exodus. Once she arrived, a Chi was standing sentry as the rise in League attacks were only going to continue, and she asked if he could send her on her way to an area out of sight outside Charlie's.

"Enjoy the ride," the man said, the red creeping around her skin. The second her feet lifted off of the floor, Cassidy's boots reconnecting with asphalt from outside as she finally took in a breath. It was strange how much every person's magic felt different, even within the same Origin. Chase's magic compared to the man who sent her to the bar felt like night and day to her. It took her a moment to have the pulse through her body fade away but within a minute of arriving outside of Charlie's, she felt normal.

It took her about five minutes to walk up to the door to the establishment she nearly grew up in, grinning when some of the regulars started hooting and hollering when she entered Charlie's door. "Alright, alright, I wasn't gone that long!" Cassidy laughed, brushing her hair behind her ears and making her way to the bar, nodding to Charlie with a soft smile. It was the best gesture she could manage, knowing that Chase had played with his head in order for her to keep her job.

58 Epsilon

Minutes in and it had seemed as if she had never left. Beers were being slung back and forth, regulars showing up by the handfuls just to get a glimpse of her working behind the bar again. Many of them passed on their condolences, commented on how great she looked and how much she was missed. The gratitude was overwhelming but a nagging feeling in the back of her mind made her welcome all the attention. It was the first time in awhile that she had thought about her dad or even her normal life. A twinge of guilt rolled through her body, her heart skipping a beat as her stomach churned in knots at the thought. She knew he'd understand why she abandoned her thoughts about him. Mr. Hawkins would be the first person to tell her to dive in head first with what the Exodus had to offer her. No one would blame her.

"So, are you a celebrity that I just don't know about or...?" a voice she couldn't recognize said, coming from the end of the bar. The man had brown hair, stubble covering his entire face and a fairly muscular build but not overwhelming. The dark beer sat in front of him, half drank from his order not even an hour prior. Cassidy didn't catch a name from the man but his green eyes were the most memorable thing about him. They mirrored her Epsilon color perfectly.

"Just someone who was gone for a while. But I'm back now and these guys don't know what to do with themselves," Cassidy laughed, walking down to where the man was perched at the bar, leaning back against the wood. "And, no offense, but yours is a face that I don't recognize," she added, looking him over for a moment.

"That's because I'm new. Or, well, sort of. Moved into the old Frankfurt place off of Holiday Drive about three weeks ago," he said, taking a swig from his glass. "Sebastian," he said, holding out his hand to her.

Cassidy managed a nod and a warm smile while he explained himself and watched as he outstretched his hand to her. She involuntarily chewed on the inside of her lip for a moment as she thought about taking his hand. All of her nerves for the night were swimming under her skin. And, while to most, it was merely a handshake, to Cassidy it was the first physical activity with just a human since experiencing her powers. Could she keep her magic buried under her skin long enough to shake a hand? Unsure of the answer, Cassidy picked up her glass of coke and cheers it against Sebastian's instead, laughing slightly.

"Cassidy, glad to meet ya. If you've heard anything about me, I promise it's all not true," she teased, swallowing back her drink before setting it down.

Sebastian watched the woman in front of him for a moment, letting his tongue run over the bottom of his lips, savoring the taste of the beer still lingering there before leaning back on his bar stool. It was obvious that she was against shaking his hand—which he didn't take to heart but he definitely remembered it.

"I promise I'll keep that in mind now that I've finally met you. These guys talk you up around here," he said, gesturing his bottle towards all of the regulars in the bar. Cassidy's cheeks warmed and a soft chuckle rumbled in the back of her throat before she grabbed up a new beer for him and sat it next to his current one. Sebastian nodded in thanks before playing with the now emptied bottle.

"So, I guess it'd be too forward of me to ask why you were gone for so long?" he questioned, arching a furrowed brow up at her for a moment.

Cassidy was slightly surprised to get the question, knowing that Charlie wouldn't be asking her such questions after Chase convinced him with his Origin. She knew that it was coming, in the back of her mind but she didn't know if she was ready to answer it.

"Uh," she said, straightening her stance and glancing around, hoping and praying that someone was suddenly at the bar and needed her for a minute or two. Of course, her eyes managed to not land on one single person and she started to gnaw on the inside of her lip in a nervous tick.

"You don't have to answer," he said, moments after watching her demeanor change at the question, clearing his throat to grab her attention. Cassidy managed a small yet gentle smile before she dismissed his concern by shaking her head.

"No, no, it's fine. I—uh—just haven't really talked about it since it all happened," she said, placing her hands on the bar and leaning against it. "My Dad recently passed away. I had to take time off to deal with his things and... process," she said, crossing her arms over her chest in a protective manner, feeling the heat of her hand against the fabric of her shirt. Her heart started to pound, causing her to worry for another minute as she swallowed back the want and need to turn to her Origin. No one had asked about her father after she woke up from the accident. Family was informed but many of the things were handled by the Exodus and Cassidy was forever grateful for that. The weeks spent mourning her father were covered by plunging herself into Epsilon and learning everything she could from her new abilities. If she were being honest, she didn't even get a moment to truly mourn her father. Cassidy felt the guilt cascade over her, swallowing it back as best she could, remembering where she was. "Sorry," she said, shrugging her shoulders and trying to have a strong facade in front of the patron.

"Don't be," Sebastian said, looking her over. "I think that's a pretty guaranteed reason to still be a little emotional." he said, taking another swig of his beer before adding. "I'm sorry, by the way. You said you hadn't talked about it since it happened so I'm sure you haven't been told that yet."

Cassidy's breath slightly hitched in her throat. The strange man in front of her was absolutely right. She'd been so worked up in training and becoming a better fighter, a better Epsilon that she simply bypassed everything that came with mourning, even condolences.

"Thank you," she said softly, lifting her glass for yet

another cheers and excusing herself from Sebastian, working quickly on a few other people who came up and had orders.

About four people deep into pouring up drinks and there was a man who was extremely inebriated, yelling at Cassidy for one reason or the other but mainly because she refused to serve him anything else for the evening.

"I'm sorry Sir, you'll just need to sit down over there and I can call you a cab or you can call someone to pick you up but you're done drinkin' for the night," she reaffirmed, her left hand gripping the bar counter and the brief swirl of green igniting around the back of her palm. It swirled as her composure lessened through the drunken insults and it wasn't until about fifteen seconds later that she noticed she had conjured her Origin to the surface. Her right hand clasped over top her left, the magic getting snuffed out as she instructed the man to go sit back at his table for the last time. The man eventually conceded, mumbling under his breath about how wretched she was and stumbling back to his chair as she called him a cab. It was very reminiscent of what happened to her father on his last day of his life but she swallowed back that thought as best she could.

While no one seemed to notice the Origin magic spin around her hand, that didn't mean that no one actually saw it. One managed to, hiding his grin when he saw it before she managed to make it back to standing in front of him.

"Sorry 'bout that," she said, leaning back against the wood of the bar before sighing. "Some guys just get that alcohol armor on them and think they're invincible," she said, shrugging.

"Nah, you did your job, it was pretty good," he commended her, finishing off the second beer that she had served him before pulling out the cash from his wallet and tossing it on top the bar. "Maybe next time I'll be able to spend my whole time here chatting with you," he teased, a grin crossing his features as he pulled his coat on and stood in front of her. He had probably ¾ of a foot on her and Cassidy had to peer up at him to keep eye contact.

"Gotta head out before you become the younger version of him?" she teased, tossing her head towards the older gentleman who was just very loud in front of her. Sebastian chuckled, running his hand through his hair before shoving both of his hands into his pockets and shrugging.

"Who knows, maybe I already am him. You've just met me," he teased which got an eye roll from Cassidy and a laugh. It was playful and distracting and surprisingly welcomed. Not that Cassidy felt trapped inside with Chase and the rest of the Exodus... it was just that she felt like herself suddenly. Without even realizing it, she slid back into the normalcy of being a regular woman in a regular job without the needed hassle of training or learning or studying her craft. It wasn't that she hated being magical; it was far from that. She just wanted balance.

Sebastian could see that his words struck her, although he couldn't understand why him being playful affected her so strongly. His brow arched, a curious gaze falling over her and before long, Cassidy squished her nose and ran her hand over her face with laughter, grabbing up the beer bottles and clearing his space.

"Sorry, just kinda zoned out for a sec," she said, trying to calm her red cheeks as best she could. "it was nice meeting you, Sebastian, regardless of whom you might be." She nodded, cracking a smile.

Sebastian smirked and nodded in turn, moving backwards towards the door a few steps. "Pleasure was mine, Cassidy," he said, flicking a few fingers into the air as a quick wave before departing the bar.

A few steps out of the bar and Sebastian pulled out his phone, getting down a few contacts before he could hear the soft scuffle of shoes behind him. The noise was clear, a tell that someone was eagerly tailing him right when he left the bar.

"It's not nice to stalk, you know... Brother."

Chase leaned out of the shadows where he was walking behind Sebastian, catching the few paces they had between one another. It was obvious that the men were close in age, perhaps even twins if that were possible. Characteristics were similar: brown hair in various lengths, similar heights and builds but the biggest difference were Sebastian's emerald green eyes and Chase's deep pools of blue. Chase seemed to be more put together, a bad boy edge that had been cleaned and quaffed to perfection whereas Sebastian just screamed *bad*. The distinction became more apparent as the pair walked side by side, Chase standing upright and alert and Sebastian more relaxed and nonchalant. For brothers, they were world's apart.

"Is that the best way to welcome a brother you haven't seen in some time, Bas?" Chase questioned, glancing over to his brother but his body seemed tense, almost ready to strike should the opportunity present itself. Sebastian chuckled, rolling his shoulders until the muscles felt loose and met Chase's gaze.

"It's not like you're exactly inviting me over when you have a free minute," Sebastian said, shrugging his shoulders. It was obvious that the two were estranged however, it wasn't obvious why.

Chase sighed, continuing to walk next to his brother as he pushed through his connection with Cassidy to check on her. When he was settled that she was fine, he continued his conversation.

"That's not my fault and you know it," he remarked, watching Sebastian process his words.

"-Listen, if you followed me to give me a stern talking to, you can save it. I'm not drinkin' the koolaide." Sebastian used his right arm away from Chase to finish his text message from earlier without his brother seeing it.

"There's nothing to drink, Bas. You're being ridiculous. All you have to do is admit that you were misled, that Geneva twisted your thoughts and beg for forgiveness. I can put in a good word with the Chancellor to let you back in," he said, trying to reason with him, if only for a moment. Their relationship had grown volatile over the years but he was still his brother and family mattered to him, regardless of what Sebastian thought.

"I already told you to save it, Chase. Believe what you want to believe but the evidence I presented was true. Whether you want to believe me or not is your call. I didn't seek you out, you followed after me. And, if I recall correctly, the last time you saw me, you tried to kill me." Sebastian snarled but the sound didn't affect his posture. He still appeared relaxed.

"You broke the laws. Not me. You turned your back on the Exodus, on the Chancellor, on me. So, don't you go start playing the victim card." Chase clenched his fists that were hidden in his jacket, trying to keep the anger brimming under his skin as best he could. He didn't need Cassidy feeling that he was worked up and he definitely didn't need Sebastian to notice.

"You've got to....you've got to be kidding me! You still blame me? After all this time?! You're blind! You are a sheep who's being led to mother fucking slaughter and you have absolutely no idea! Because, you won't listen! And you know what? That shit ain't on me. I tried to get you to follow me and instead you ratted to the Chancellor and got Holly killed. She was our sister, Chase!" His voice was booming and thankfully they'd taken enough space away from the busy street so that onlookers didn't get wind of their conversation. At the mention of Holly, Chase's hand ignited a bright red and soared energy into Sebastian's chest, lifting him up and tossing him roughly fifty feet away from him against a light pole. Sebastian groaned when his body collapsed against it, forcing himself up to his feet with a laugh.

"So that's how this goes, huh? Origin over blood?" Sebastian asked, brow arched towards his brother at his question. "Guess by now, I shouldn't be surprised. You picked the Exodus over me before, why would I think it would be any different now?" he spat out, taking a few steps to close the distance between the two of them. "I just have one question for ya... did you ever even believe me? Or, did you know from the beginning you were going to side with the Chancellor's story of how the story played out?" Sebastian stood roughly twenty feet in front of Chase, hands at the ready to attack should he need to.

"You're my baby brother, of course I wanted to believe you but... you weren't yourself. You were letting the Origin consume you and when the Chancellor walked in on you with Holly dead... what else was I supposed to believe?!" Chase was yelling now, confronting his brother once and for all about what happened that night.

"Fucking believe me! That's what you're supposed to do! You don't just assume what you hear to be true! Listen to all the fucking rumors that spread about you! I didn't kill Holly.

She meant more to me than anything. We were supposed to protect her, how could you say that I killed her!" Sebastian's voice was hurt, the anger waning only for the brief minute of listening to his brother admit that he thought that he killed Holly. They'd been so heated in fighting the past few months that they hadn't had this argument yet.

"Because you got addicted to it. You needed more of it and what better way than creating someone to be joined to that you already loved! You wanted her triggered so you took her life, hoped to revive her but you couldn't bring her back. You couldn't save her. And when the Chancellor found you out, you were exiled and you started to run with the leeches. What else am I supposed to think?!" Chase was fuming at this point, trying desperately to keep his anger in check long enough to get through the conversation with his brother.

"I told you then... when I came in, Holly was already dead and the Chancellor was standing over her. He framed me! And the League aren't leeches. They're trying to expose the Exodus for what they truly are. You're just too blind to accept it," Sebastian growled, the red sparking over his hand, closing his eyes as he tried to focus through the addiction to the magic and focus on Chase. It was seconds before his hand was wrapped around Chase's throat, hoisting him into the air. "Grow a damn pair and wake up," he said, squeezing his hand harder against Chase's windpipe. "And remember, I did this for you," he finished, letting the red magic envelope his body as he disappeared, leaving Chase on the ground. His hand went to his throat, rubbing away the raw feeling against his trachea as he attempted to breathe. Now that Sebastian was gone, his anger seemed to settle and he could feel the one thing he was ignoring the entire time Sebastian was there. Cassidy's fear.

It was nearly crippling now, Chase's heart racing at the emotions that began to cascade around him. It took him every fiber of his being to breathe as he tried to figure out where she might be. He could picture through her mind that she was outside of Charlie's, walking towards a safe distance away so that she could call on a Chi guard to send her back to the Exodus. When he was comfortable that no regular human could see him teleport to her, he did.

Within a second, Chase appeared within an arm's distance of Cassidy, the bright red fading away right when he went to speak.

"Cass?" he questioned, grabbing her arm to have her look at him. He didn't see anyone circling her or following her. For all he knew, she was just scared for another reason. Regardless, it was strong enough to be filtered through their bond. "Cassidy!"

Cassidy glanced up at Chase, as if she were in a daze. It took her a moment before she could connect her eyes to his and Chase could tell that something was wrong. Something big.

"What's wrong?" he demanded, grabbing hold of both her shoulders and staring down at her. "Damnit, Cass, answer me!" Chase couldn't hide the fear in his voice as their link connection began to fade, the fear waning from the bond until all Chase could feel was himself.

"You're brother is one amazing Chi," Cassidy said, her expressionless face turning into a grin as the base of her hair slowly transformed into a bright silvery blonde, revealing Geneva standing in front of him. "Even managed to trick your bond into thinking I was her," she mused, leaning forward and snapping her jaw at him with a playful growl. "Don't look so down, we'll take care of her. We promise." Geneva's grin turned frightening as Chase's eyes narrowed, grabbing her and tossing her to the ground with his human strength instead of his Chi abilities.

"Where is she?!" Chase yelled, the red swirling around his skin and practically begging to be released. "You tell me where she is right now, Geneva, and I'll make sure your death is quick," he spat out, quickly picking her up and pinning her against the wall.

Geneva laughed at his feeble excuse of being terrifying. It really didn't phase her at all; the way Chase reacted. She would gladly die for the League. It was a cause that she believed in with every fiber of her being and she would gladly take down one of the Chancellor's favorite players. "Don't wear your emotions so on your sleeve, Chase," she croaked out from the pressure against her windpipe. "It isn't like you to get so wrapped up so quickly."

Geneva looked over Chase. It was obvious that there was some kind of history that was shared between the two of them. It didn't seem romantic but it was clear that they were once close. Most importantly, they were initiated into their origins at the same ceremony. They didn't pick the same homes but that didn't mean that they didn't have a bond. It wasn't as close as Chase and Cassidy's happened to be but it was there nonetheless.

"That's funny, coming from you." Chase pressed into her, ready for her to try and use her Origin against him. If Cassidy was help in any sort of way, it helped him learn what most Epsilons would start off with in an attack. "Just tell me where your took her, Gen. She has no part of this."

"All of this has to do with her. Don't you get that? Don't you see? If we can't get Sebastian to convince you, you better believe I'll find a way to get the doe eyed brunette to snap you out of this." Geneva's hands finally turned a bright emerald green, but instead of the heat that he had become accustomed to from Cassidy, the parts of his body that were touching Geneva started to become ice cold to frozen within miliseconds. It was clear that the two Epsilons he knew varied greatly in strength.

Chase was forced to let her go, the red seeping his hands and passing through her head, sending sharp pains telekinetically which caused Geneva to cry out. Her hands went up into her hair, gripping her head to try and rid the pain as she screamed. The green erupted from her body as the wind lifted Chase off of the ground and hurled him away from her, breaking connection enough for the pain to subside in her head.

"You'd have to kill me to give her up," Geneva said, managing to get to her feet and wipe away the blood that started to fall freely from her nose—both an indication of intense Origin use and the damage Chase caused to her brain.

"Gladly," Chase said, conjuring a wave of psychotic attacks to her, Geneva managing to parry each of his attacks as they came her way. Before Chase could go again, Geneva had him wrapped up in the Earth, the ground having hold of him and constricting him every which way.

"Be mindful of your attacks. Your girl is gonna need her strength and she's connected to you... for now." Geneva winked, egging on the rocks that had hold of Chase to strengthen their grip. "Until next time, Chase," she whispered, leaning up and locking eyes with him for a moment, the hatred reflected in his and the desperation lurking deep in her own.

And, like she was never even there, Chase was by himself once more. The Earth was hardened around him, binding him to it like he had always been there. He felt suffocated and with each breath, he felt more and more confined. While the bond to Cassidy was masked—primarily in part to whatever the League was trying to do to her—she managed to push out snippets of feelings. Fear. Anger. Aggression. She was too preoccupied to pass along anything of true importance but Chase could care less at the exact moment. The fact that he could still feel her meant that the League hadn't severed their connection and that was what mattered.

Chase groaned out in pain, trying to free himself just enough to be able to use his Origin to get him completely out of the ground that nearly ate him whole. Because of his very active night in using his Origin, he needed to calm his breathing and heart rate before he could teleport anywhere of great distance.

Minutes later, he was out of the ground, several cuts

bleeding down his arms but he was alive and that was enough for him. It was as if his body was on autopilot at that moment, transporting him back to the Exodus to inform the Chancellor and the rest of the people what had happened. The first night of Cassidy leaving the Exodus—on recommendations of Chase himself—and she managed to get kidnapped by the enemy. It was going to be a wonderful report.

"Cassidy was taken," Chase blurted out when he reached the Chancellor's study, pushing the doors open. He was covered in dust, blood, sweat and the Chancellor didn't appear to share pity in his appearance.

"What?" he asked, peering at the man who was standing in front of him, almost holding back a laugh.

"She went to work tonight, I told her she should go. Have a normal night out. I was watching her the entire time... until I saw Sebastian and I—"

"So, what you're telling me is the first night your charge left our protective walls and you didn't think it was weird that Sebastian was there?" the Chancellor snapped off, his voice steady but it was obvious he didn't approve of Chase's handling of the case.

Chase swallowed hard, clasping his hands in front of himself with a nod. "He distracted me long enough for Geneva to step in and grab her and place herself in Cassidy's stead. My bond brought me to her instead of Cassidy when I reached out through it," he said, his tone defeated but still full of anger.

"That means Sebastian's abilities have simply grown stronger since the last time we saw him, perhaps even stronger than your own."

The Chancellor welcomed the chiding remark against Chase. At this point, he deserved to be punished like a father would to a son. He took a few steps to stand in front of Chase, his gaze unwavering.

"I do not care what you have to do. Find the girl, retrieve her and kill whomever you have to to get it done. Another minute she is there and there is no telling what they may try to brainwash her against," the Chancellor reminded him.

The second the words left the Chancellor's mouth, Chase's gaze fell. Sebastian, Cassidy, hell, even Geneva was changed by the League. Exile changed a person enough but when they formed a coalition to ensure the death and the destruction of the Exodus, it had changed them.

The only thing he could hope for was that he could find Cassidy before it was too late. God, he hoped so.

Chapter 9

The metallic taste spread within her mouth like wildfire. At first it was simply a taste and before she knew it, it had filled her entire mouth. Cassidy didn't even remember getting hit, if she were honest but the taste was a blatant sign. Her wrists were bound in front of her, the bindings digging into her wrists with each twist and move that she tried to escape. Her hair was matted against her forehead, congealed to her sweat and the trail of blood that had happened from when Geneva captured her. She hated herself for falling for such an obvious trick to begin with.

It happened so quickly and she couldn't explain why she felt so compelled to help. A woman was being pushed around in an alley outside of Charlie's. Cassidy wouldn't have even noticed if the young girl hadn't called out in agony to help her. Her nerves were on edge and she was on pins and needles, terrified and outraged that a young woman was getting attacked near her work.

"Hey! Leave her alone!" Cassidy yelled, moving down the alley towards the girl and the hooded figure that was accosting her. She didn't think about why the figure was cloaked other than the fact that it was obvious something nefarious was about to go down. If only Cassidy knew how right her thought process was.

"Please, help me!" the female voice from the alley rang out, the woman sinking to the ground and Cassidy swallowed back the green magic that was begging to break the surface. If Chase was good for anything, it was the fact that he had been teaching her how to hold her own in a fight.

"Buddy, you heard the girl!" Cassidy's voice rang, running to pull the guy off of her but when her hand touched the hooded figure, the man vanished under her touch. Cassidy took in a quick breath, gazing to the woman who was yelling. The minute her eyes connected with her, she vanished just the same as the hooded figure and now Cassidy was deep in the alleyway all by herself.

"This is not good," she mumbled, running her hand over her hair to get it out of her face, turning around in the alley to confirm she was actually alone. "Maybe I'm going nuts," she added, fiddling with her keys as she walked to get out of the alley. It was at that point where a dark male, approximately six foot tall stood at the entryway, hands glowing a bright orange color. "Sigma," she whispered to herself, her mind running through all the possible attack options she had with a member of the necromancy Origin. It was the first time she'd ever even met a Sigma Origin member, let alone face it. There was a big difference between what a book taught her to do and real life.

Before a word could leave her mouth, Cassidy felt the wave of despair cross over her, her hairs standing on end. The alley appeared darker, black entities encircling around her and they were terrifying enough to keep her grounded in place.

"What do you want?" The words fumbled from her lips,

body rigid but begging to shake as the fear left her frozen. The emotions were so strong that she was unable to conjure her Origin to her skin.

"To show you the truth," The man boomed, dreadlocks down to his shoulders and at least three times the size of Cassidy. He took enough steps to close the space between them and pressed his hand to her, seeping the orange into her skin. "Don't fight it," he whispered, the dark souls surrounding them and transporting them underground, into a Sigma channeling room. In League headquarters.

"I still think bringing her here was a little much. And... with such theatrics, we look like the bad guys!" Sebastian complained out of earshot of Cassidy who was unconscious on the ground under a holding sigil. The room she was in was seeped in Sigma magic and while that strengthened any Sigma, it weakened any other Origin. She was unable to reach out through her bond or even through her Origin to try and contact someone else. She was captive.

"Oh, settle down. She's fine and it's best to try and reason with her before your brother and the others manage to get their hands into her even more. We all know who she could be. She needs to be on our side," Geneva said, leaning against a rather ornate table, books strewn open with pens outlining specific elements on the pages. The headquarters was not as opulent as the Exodus', that was evident. The rooms looked relatively old but not terribly special. Inside the space were a few bookshelves full of texts and the room that they were all standing in was a rotunda of sorts with five off shoot rooms along with one long hallway. Each door had a sigil on it in various colors, coordinating with the Origin that it strengthened inside. The rooms were similar to the ones within the Exodus, obviously there to help heighten the magic of the supposed traitors. Sebastian was sitting over the arm of one of the chairs closest to the Chi channeling room, Caleb, the large African American Sigma that had captured Cassidy was standing nearest to the door of his Origin, often glancing over his shoulder to ensure that Cassidy hadn't woke up just yet. The other two people in the room, Flora, an exiled Omicron, stood tall with long jet black hair and piercing silver blue eyes. Her face was rather gaunt, each one of her attributes sharper than the next. And then, next to her, was Bryan, a Delta with striking resemblance to the Chancellor. It was apparent that the most recent exiled members of the Exodus meant a lot to many of the remaining members.

"You don't have to remind me as to who she might be, Gen. I know damn well who you made me trigger," Sebastian snapped back, running his hands over his face to try and hide how badly they were shaking. Sebastian clearly didn't look nearly as calm and steady as he did when facing his brother earlier and one could only assume it was due to the Chi energy that was surging under his skin. Making Geneva appear to be Cassidy took a lot out of a normal Chi, one that wasn't addicted to using magic. Sebastian had tried to dial back his Origin use for the past few months since leaving the Exodus. Being condemned as the killer of his sister, using magic for mundane tasks, pushing himself... the were all signs that he was heading down a path that many didn't return from. Geneva had managed to help him over the weeks but nothing helped when he used this heavily. Not only that but this was the first time since the accident that he had managed to meet Cassidy. It was no secret that the League had orchestrated Cassidy's death, even the Exodus had supported that claim but no one knew exactly who had done it until now. Geneva needed to ensure that Sebastian was still playing the game that she had set forth and the best way to test that theory was to have him kill for her. She had hoped that he'd be the one to jump in and save her, to forcibly trigger and join with her, but his pesky brother Chase beat her to the punch. There was still time to tilt Cassidy's ideals, though.

Sebastian leaned up in his chair and buried his face into his hands, letting out a shaky sigh before taking in a new breath and letting it out. This wasn't the time or the place for him to start losing it.

Geneva narrowed her eyes towards the comment that Sebastian made, shrugging it off before peering over Caleb's shoulder towards Cassidy who was sprawled out on the floor.

"Be mindful of your quippy nature, Williams," Gen said, raising a brow at Sebastian, using the greeting that she had previously used to greet Chase when she attacked Cassidy at her home.

"Aye aye, Captain," Sebastian said, rolling his eyes as he stood, shoving his hands in his pockets and shrugging his shoulders. "You guys don't need me for this part, yeah? I'm gonna try and get some sleep before the Exodus comes barking down our door trying to find their girl," Sebastian said, walking closer to where Caleb was standing and feeling the call of the Sigma room to him, begging for his life force to enter the room and allow it to feed the Origin. Sigmas were a terrifying breed for any of the other origins and most stayed clear of them in general but Sebastian could respect the magic. Everyone had something to be afraid of, it wasn't their choice to be blanketed in such a dark magic.

"We can handle her." Caleb nodded, leaning against the doorway and glancing at the woman who they had captive. "Crazy to think that she could be the key to ending all of this," he said with a laugh, Sebastian clasping his back and squeezing the top of his shoulder.

"Just make sure she survives," he said with a nod and Caleb agreed. If both sides could agree on anything, it was that Cassidy Hawkins was the one person they needed to survive.

"Don't be so doom and gloom, Sebastian! We'll take care of her," Gen called out as Sebastian started to walk away down the hall, head hung low as his feet carried him back to his room on the other side of the headquarters.

"What a worry wart," Gen mumbled before clapping her hands together and gazing at Caleb. "Well, we all know that I can't go in there and the fact that we're the same Origin means she can't go into Epsilon with me without growing stronger. So, either Sigma or Delta can handle her, you two boys take your pick." She grinned, tapping her fingers on the table in front of her. A few moments passed as the boys stayed silent before she pounded her fist on the table and then sighed once more. "Come on, one of you needs to volunteer," she mused, playing with the ends of her bright blonde hair.

"I can do it. I already have her stable," Caleb said with a shrug, watching as Cassidy started to stir on the floor in the Sigma room. "And, Origin sharing or not, you definitely wouldn't be leading this. She's already terrified of you," Caleb said with a laugh while Gen narrowed her eyes.

"Well, it's your job to get her to change her mind about that, alright? We need her," she said, twirling her fingers on the table and conjuring a mini tornado about the size of her hand, forcing it back and forth to entertain her as she waved Caleb on. "Go on, go on, no use in waiting. Longer we wait, longer they have to find her and rescue her," she said with a sigh, continuing to play with her windstorm she had conjured.

Caleb nodded, turning on his heel and stepping into the Sigma room, his heart settling the moment he entered and his hairs standing on end as the home of his magic surrounded him. He felt every fiber of his being all at once, closing his eyes and soaking in the moment before turning to Cassidy who was starting to come to on the ground.

"Cassidy," he whispered, her head lifting to his voice as she recognized it from the alleyway. She tried to conjure her Origin to her hand but the Sigma sigil kept her from being able to use.

"What the hell..." she mumbled, her eyes still adjusting to the light in the room and she could feel the unsettling feeling grow in her stomach. It was as if the Epsilon magic was drained from her body. As if, she were normal.

"What did you do to me?!" Cassidy cried out, scurrying to her feet as she stared at her hands, glancing to the walls and above her on the roof before landing on Caleb. She knew the sigils enough to understand that she was in a channeling room but she'd never been in another Origin's room before and definitely did not like what she was feeling. She felt empty.

"It's merely a precaution. We can't have you trying to attack us... or leave," Caleb said, waving his hand away which caused two dark figures with not apparent features other than the fact that they were nearly soul sucking. They were lost souls in the middle of limbo, acting to the beck and call of Caleb on a wave of his hand. It may not be a terribly active ability but they caused a mountain of dread to well up within her. He waved his hands and had the figures clasp around her wrists, ridding her of her bindings and sending the creatures back away from her. Cassidy's skin was pure white except for the bit of blood on her face and her wrists from struggling.

"Why am I here?" she ask, wrapping her arms around her and edging away from the figures, her eyes darting back and forth from them to Caleb. Her fear was palpable, even bits and pieces of it pushing and trying to get through to her bond with Chase.

"Because you're being lied to," he said simply, grabbing a chair and sitting on it as he watched her body tremble. It was exhausting to watch her shiver and quake, especially when he hadn't done anything yet but he was used to it by now. Sigmas in general were used to being feared. "The Exodus is not what you think it is, Cassidy. And I'm sorry we had to do all of this to show you but it was the only way."

Cassidy laughed. It was an honest laugh, not one given out of spite. She truly thought that his statement was downright laughable. The only way to let her know about a group she had came to love was by capturing her? In what world did that make sense.

"Are you kidding me right now? You think I can trust anything you say while you have me locked up? Do you not see the flaws there?" she questioned, trying to shake away the nagging fear that the figures threw on her.

Caleb nodded, a wave of orange erupted over the room and the figures took a step back, giving Cassidy some breathing room. She couldn't help the heavy sigh of relief that fell from her body when the figures backed off a few feet. Necromancy never seemed so terrifying until right now.

"If you think that I'm going to believe a word that you say, you're a fool," Cassidy said, hands clenching down at her sides as she begged her Origin to break the surface.

"It won't work. Sigma magic is the only entity that thrives here. I don't want to have to use my powers against you but I will if I have to," he said, more as a reminder than anything else.

"I get it. You're terrifying. Can you just get the point already?" Cassidy spat out, taking a few steps back to get even further away from the figures that were stalking the edges of where she was standing.

"The Exodus... their motives aren't as clear and clean as they've been letting you understand. Every person in this building have seen the deplorable things they will do to keep their way of life continuing on. The rules that they created... they're the ones breaking them, not us." Caleb let the orange pulse over his hands, watching Cassidy's reactions as he told her what he knew. Everything relied on her accepting the actual truth.

But, she couldn't. The Exodus had granted her a home, a family. It had become everything to her so quickly that a few words from a stranger couldn't seal her doubt.

"But why? Why go through the pomp and circumstance to define this group of people, this fellowship, and base it all on a lie? Wouldn't it be simpler just to have the Chis convince the new members that the Exodus is the end all, be all? Wouldn't that make it easier to control all of us?" Cassidy questioned, pacing in front of Caleb as she thought through what the man said. It really was too far fetched to even be plausible. Cassidy was right. The Chancellor and the rest of the Exodus were too strong to just let them run around with their free will in tact. If they had ulterior motives, it would be far too simple to keep them all in check.

"You tell me. Which is better: a willing army or one subdued into thinking that the cause that they're fighting for is the right one? Having a completely faithful army at your disposal with none the wiser, to protect the family that they have cultivated, don't you think they've done a bang up job? The Exodus didn't always exist. There was a time in the history of our origins that people just existed with these abilities. The bones of our past are rooted into the Exodus but they don't have everyone's best interest at heart. It might seem like they sacrifice the few for the many but it's more like what the many can do for the few." Caleb's voice grew elevated as he spoke. Each person had a different reason for being exiled from the Exodus. The feeling of being striped away from the connection that a member had made was a pain he never wished upon another person for the rest of their life.

Cassidy had to hand it to him. He made the entire scenario make sense, in a way. But Cassidy had spent a good portion of the past two months living and breathing with Exodus members. She could tell that they were genuine in thought and actions. The League had nothing to lose and everything to gain by convincing Cassidy of what the true purpose of the League was. And that fact, very much like the reasoning Caleb gave for not brainwashing the Exodus members, was what terrified her. What if she was wrong? What if she was supporting a group that was against what she had grown to love over the past two months? Could she survive losing her family all over again?

"Say you're right. Say I believe you. What do you expect me to do about it? I'm... so new. Why do I matter in all of this? I get that flipping a newbie will be easier than a veteran but this seems specific. Like, I'm needed for this in some major way," she said, sizing him up. She knew there was no way that she could possibly take him on in a Sigma channeling room but there had to be some way out of the compound. Chase had to be looking for her by this point, right?

"It's who you are. Or, at least, who your parents are," Caleb said and Cassidy's heart leapt into her throat at his comment, almost buckling her to her knees.

"What about my parents," she muttered, chewing on the inside of her lip as she waited on bated breath. It'd been so long since she had seen her mother, it cursed her that she sometimes couldn't remember what she looked like. And, her father's death was still at the forethought of her mind and fresh. It wasn't that long ago that she was going to his for weekly dinner and now he was rotting six feet underground.

"Your mother wasn't who you thought she was. She was one of the first," Caleb said, glancing around the room and then out towards the door before looking back to Cassidy. "She started the League," he said, crossing his arms over his chest as the words hit her stronger than she ever thought possible.

"No," she said, shaking her head and trying to hide the tremble in her voice. "My mother was... sick. She'd been battling that for years. And instead of asking for help, she resorted to another mea—"

"Autopsy said she OD'd, right? But, the toxicology came back as inconclusive?" Caleb said and Cassidy's words trailed off, distracting her when he hit her with the truth.

"How did you know th—"

"Because, it's the easiest way to kill one of us without making it look like a murder. A few of us have issues with it over the years. Addiction to your Origin can be intoxicating. You feel like you can't breathe without using. You become lost, incoherent. You babble and you lash out. It looks like you've gone mental but in all reality, you've just lost yourself to the never ending power inside you."

Caleb stared at his hands and dropped the large dark figures that were circling Cassidy. She was still a threat but he felt comfortable enough to let her sit in the room without being threatened. "She'd been exiled from the Exodus for a few weeks by the time of her death. She'd seen too much, found out too many secrets over time and that was too dangerous. She was more of a liability and with her problems that already had grown over the years, staging her death was easy. Overloading her with magic was probably the easiest and magic doesn't show up on an autopsy.

"So, while you thought that your mother had gone batshit and just gave up, we all knew differently. Some of us believed the story that was sold to us. Some could see through the utter bullshit. When it was your father feeding us the bullshit, it was harder for many to deny it as fact."

"My father? My Da- my Dad had nothing to do with this world... he- he wouldn't be able to hide something like this from me. He... you're wrong. I don't know who told you this story but you're wrong." Cassidy shook her head vehemently, unable to believe what Caleb was spitting out now. It was just more propaganda to get her to turn against the only family she had grown to love.

"Not him. Not Mr. Hawkins. When your mother died, there was no way to ensure you could be protected, no way of knowing that you would be able to stay safe with all those out there who would target you. You weren't triggered yet and your mother wanted to make sure that only happened if you were fated to have these abilities. She didn't want that choice taken from you.

"So, the Exodus did the only thing that they could do without triggering you. They found a man in a nearby town, used a Chi to implant a backstory capable of explaining your entire history. Then, the Chi was forced to fix your memories, erase the Exodus history and implant one that would keep you safe and secure. All at the request of your father," Caleb said, leaning forward in his chair and resting his elbows on his knees, leaning forward and clasping his hands together while she processed the information presented to her.

Her history, her memories, they were all, supposedly, fabricated. She couldn't remember her mother, she couldn't remember her real father... and the man she thought was her Dad was just another man off the road. How could this all be true?

"So then, if this is all... say I was to even try to believe everything that you're saying. Who, then is—"

"Your father?" Caleb interrupted her again, nodding his head when he realized where her thought process was going. "Well, that one is easy. You've met him. Your father is the Chancellor."

Chapter 10

assidy laughed a guttural laugh once more. It resonated in the pit of her stomach, reverberating up her windpipe as she couldn't control it. Her hand lifted to her lips to stifle it, shaking her head back and forth at the utter craziness of what Caleb tried to tell her.

"You're saying... that the man who is supposedly the worst out of the Exodus is my father, and that he had my mother killed and my memories wiped so that I would... live a normal life?" Cassidy laughed again, trying to picture the Chancellor in her head, desperately trying to piece together if she looked anything like him or not.

"At first he couldn't kill her. Your mother set the precedence within our community. She was the first one to be exiled and she was kicked out instead of killed because she was your mother and meant so much to the Chancellor. However, when she started screaming about his indiscretions, about how the Chancellor was creating an army and forcibly triggered dozens every month, she suddenly ended up dead." Caleb licked his lips and leaned back in his chair. "Your mother had her issues under control. The only reason she was so overwhelmed with her abilities in the first place was because what your father was making her do. She was a Chi and one heck of a Chi at that. She had shown him that someone close to the Chancellor was supposedly going to fulfil the prophecy of holding all five origins and he honestly believed that person was going to be your mother. So, he pushed her." His head sunk, hanging it low as he shook it back and forth, obviously upset by the story that he was telling. It was clear that Caleb had known her mother and was close to her. The story seemed to change him as he told it.

"When it became apparent that she could barely handle the Chi energy, let alone other origins, he wanted to trigger you. And, your mother was extremely against that. She truly believed that if you were going to be triggered, it needed to happen honestly. And, when she found out that the Chancellor was planning a way to trigger you, she lost it. She tried to bring down his Chancellor-ship, tried to turn the Exodus against him but, he painted her as an addict and showed her mercy by exiling her. But... being exiled from the Exodus is almost worse than dying. You get sick, your Origin is hard to control, you feel this emptiness inside that is unable to be quenched. And, the only way to fill the hole is to supplement with something else, so she created the League. And the rest, you know." Caleb stood, pacing in the room and hoping that she could see how honest he was trying to be.

"Why didn't he just trigger me after my mom was gone?" Cassidy asked, her voice soft as she was so tired. Arguing and being defensive didn't appear to have an effect on Caleb, she might as well try to understand what he was trying to say.

"Because, your mom was one smart cookie. In forming the League, there were too many defectors from the Exodus that he didn't have the time to worry about you. He had to keep a good face. Everyone knew that your mother didn't want you to be pushed into triggering and he couldn't just have that happen so suddenly. So, he spent his time fighting us and it wasn't until we killed you tha—"

"You killed me?" she said, her head snapping up and forcing her to swallow when he said the words. "If you respected my mother so much... why go against her dying wish?" she said, the anger brimming under her skin. She didn't understand why her mother went to such lengths to avoid her coming into her birthright but it was obvious if his story was true that that was a big part of her death.

"There comes a point in war that we're forced to do things we don't want to do. Our numbers were dwindling, we need you. You are so much more than you think you are. To have the daughter of the Chancellor side with us, someone who could possibly master all five origins and help us end the Exodus corruption... we couldn't wait any longer. And, it'd been so long since your mother died that it was either we were going to kill you or the Exodus was. We just chose to attack first."

"You make it sound so simple!" Cassidy snapped, clenching her fists and begging to be able to use her Origin against him. "I wasn't some mark or attack, that was my life you stole from me! You changed everything!" Her voice echoed out of the room and into the rotunda that the rest of the members were sitting in.

"Don't you see though, we didn't! That life was fake. Every single memory you had, even your father. All of it was a crock of shit to keep you on the back burner long enough to avoid suspicion and then bring you back into the fold. We saved you! And while we can't bring back your old memories for you, we can let you know that you're being fed a lie," Caleb sighed. He just wished that he could shake her to accept the truth that was being shown to her.

"What do you mean I can't bring back my own memories?" she questioned, pacing once more. She knew that Chase was an incredible Chi, she was sure that he would be able to undo whatever was done to her.

"When a Chi alters the mind, the memories of a person, only that Chi can undo the alteration. Chase's father was the one that altered your memories and... he died the day after your mother did," Caleb said, Cassidy's false bravado sinking the minute he spoke. The coincidences that had to have happened to orchestrate such a large scheme such as this... it was impossible. But, she couldn't take what Caleb said at face value. He wanted to sway her to his side after all.

"So, I'll never know my old life? What memories I used to have, my time with my 'real' dad, none of it?" she said, trying to hide the shake in her voice.

"Those memories died with the Chi who took them. You are the Cassidy that you will forever be, right now. You'll need to build new memories and we can help you with that. We can be the family that you're so desperate to have. Your mother created this group before she died and she would love to see you flourish here with us. And, we'd love for you to become one of us." Caleb watched her face, hoping that he could see the wheels working in his favor.

"I don't know if I can believe you," Cassidy admitted, staring at the hands in front of her and imagining the green pulsing over her skin.

"We didn't think that you would, not at first. Your true home is here. You'll learn that eventually. And, we'll be here when you're ready to come to us." Caleb licked his lips and left the room before she could say anything, leaving the door open and free to leave if she so chose to.

Cassidy's hands were shaking now that she was alone. She didn't know what to do. She didn't know who to believe. The hope that Chase was being honest with her was fading just as fast as Caleb spoke to her. What if he was just there to try and convert her? He was there at the perfect time to bring her back to life. The Chancellor was at the hospital when she came to. Everything was a lie, supposedly. Her head was screaming at her in pain as she tried to think through all of the issues that were being presented to her. If what Caleb said was true, everyone she had met had a story with her already and she'd never truly know it. Would she try and pick up wherever she left off in the Exodus or continue on in the new Cassidy Hawkins body that she knew now?

All she did know was that she needed to get out of the room.

Her feet were on auto pilot as she found her way out of the room. The room spilled out into a hallway much different design than it was earlier. There weren't other rooms that connected the other origins, the room just dumped out to a foyer with a door leading outside. Something had happened when Caleb had left the room and she couldn't figure out where she was but she knew that somehow, she was brought somewhere else. When she turned around to peer back into the Sigma channeling room, the room simply didn't exist anymore. It took her a moment to realize where she was at all. She was home. Or, at least in the house that was fabricated in her head to actually be home. The room was cold and dark, the lingering feeling of what Caleb had cast over her slowly fading away.

"This isn't home," she whispered, touching the bannister to the stairs that she had a million memories on. A million false memories.

Her heart pounded in her chest, the fear and realization she might not know who she was at all came to her mind and the green magic quickly pulsed across her skin. Cassidy's heart pounded faster, both relieved and terrified that the magic was at her disposal again. That meant that her bond should work too.

"Chase," she croaked out, her legs unable to hold her up any more as she fell to the ground, holding on to the staircase and crumpling on the last step. The red waves of magic started to ripple in front of her and not even a second after she said his name, he was standing in front of her. It was apparent that he was a nervous wreck and that he hadn't slept in some time.

"Cassidy," he said, relief rolling through their bond in heavy doses. He moved to her, picking her up and pulling her to his chest, fingers intertwining up in her hair as he took in the smell of her and closed his eyes, thankful for finding her.

"You're safe, I've got you, you're home," he whispered, rubbing her arms as she stayed silent in his arms. The problem was, she didn't know what home was anymore.

Chapter 11

The couple sat on the steps for a few minutes, eerily silent the entire time as Cassidy tried to process what all had happened. The comfort of Chase being so close was much more of a relief than it should have been and she welcomed his arms around her. It wasn't until they'd sat for a while until Chase teleported them back to the edge of the Exodus compound and then helped her back to her room. Cassidy was thankful that there wasn't a welcoming committee there to fuss over her more than Chase. She didn't need to be overwhelmed already.

"Are you okay?" he finally asked as he helped her to the couch, letting her lay on it as he paced in front of her. His eyes looked her over, trying to find any kind of marking or bruise. There was a cut on her forehead and bruising around her wrists where she had been bound, awaiting her conversation with the League. Chase's anger was palpable as he paced back in forth in front of her.

"Did you know me? When you saved me, did you know who I was, before?" Cassidy asked, her voice hoarse and raspy as she glanced up at him. "They told me everything so... I just want to know. Did you know me?"

Chase's gaze fell as he nodded, sitting on the coffee table in front of her. "We didn't know each other, not well enough at least. You kept to yourself mostly but I knew who you were. The Chancellor's daughter. So, when we tracked down the League that night and noticed so many of them converging on the town that they'd put you in, we thought that they'd be coming for you and I hoped that we'd get to you first. It was no accident that I was there that night but it was my hope that I could save you." Chase reached out to brush back her hair but she shuddered away from his touch, sinking farther back into the couch.

"So, everything..." she started, clasping her eyes closed as a few tears managed to spill over the edge, pulling her legs to her chest on the couch and letting out a shuddering breath. "Everything they said was true. This... is just some fucked up façade." She swallowed, wiping away her tears.

"No, no, Cassidy, that's not true at all," he said, his voice firm yet understanding. "The Exodus is exactly like we've told you, what you've experienced. The only lie was who your father was and I didn't tell you because I didn't think that it was right for me to tell you. Moving you away from the Exodus was what your mother wanted and Xander, he just wanted to keep you safe." He sighed, saying the Chancellor's name out loud for the first time.

Cassidy clenched her legs to her, shaking her head and burying her face into her body. There were so many lies, what was she even able to believe anymore.

"So who knows who I am?" she asked, swallowing back the fear and confusion as best she could.

"Only a few. Most of the League members memories weren't converted because we didn't want them to look for you outside of the Exodus. Most of the people you've met have no idea that you used to be living within this life before. The Chancellor, me, a few other elders for the origins, that's it," he said with a nod and Cassidy licked her lips as she accepted what he said.

"They said that the Chancellor killed my mom. That the Exodus is trying to create this army, that they're framing the League for things that the Exodus is actually doing." Cassidy sighed, pulling herself off of the couch and to the drink decanter on the kitchen counter, pouring a glass of scotch and downing it quickly. "How can I believe either of you?" She was just so lost at this point.

"Because, you trust me. You can feel what I feel. You know that I'm telling you the truth. We're bound. It's my job to protect you and I wouldn't put you in the path to be hurt," he said, standing and walking over to her, taking the glass from her hand and pouring himself one, downing it just like she had. "You scared the shit out of me, you know. I couldn't feel you anymore, couldn't search for you.. Really know how to screw with my emotions." He chuckled, sucking the last bit of scotch off of his lips before looking up at her and shaking his head.

Cassidy was ready to retort back against him until he looked up at her. It was such a strange feeling that he caused within her each time they found one another. She hated that he was just so damn good aT distracting her from the issues in her life but she secretly welcomed it too. After everything that was revealed to her tonight, a sense of security and normalcy was what she needed.

"Trust me, it wasn't my intention," she mumbled with a laugh, stealing her glass back and pouring herself another, taking a sip before watching her hands that were still shaking.

"Nerves and after effects of being in a foreign Origin channeling room," he said, nodding to her hands and grasping them in his. "keeping an Origin from a triggered person is one of the best torture methods out there. It breaks you without you ever even knowing it," he said gently, tugging her closer to him and tangling his fingers into her hair.

"You saying they were torturing me... and I thought they were going easy on me?" she whispered, her breath hitching in her throat when he pulled her closer and Chase nodded his head to her question, leaning down and pressing his lips against her own. Cassidy's skin glowed a dull green at the feeling of him against her and before she knew it, her hands were free of his own and pulling him closer to her. With his lips on her own, it was like the events of the night never happened, that she never questioned who her parents were... it was like she was normal all over again. Her hands gripped his back, nails just barely digging into his back enough to lift her even closer to him, if it were possible. Chase's hands slipped to her hips, moving to lift her to sit on the counter when Cassidy pulled away.

Her chest was heaving, her skin flushed and her lips bright red as she stared up at him. The emotions were palpable even if the bond didn't exist but with it, they were heightened tenfold.

"We can't," she whispered, her hands resting on his chest, her hair a mess and his hands now resting on the small of her back. "Not like this... not after everything today. We're hurt and... we can't," Cassidy said, peering up at him. She knew how easy it would be to let everything go and say fuck it to how her night had gone but this was important to her. Their connection wasn't one to be exploited.

Chase's breathing had calmed while she spoke, cracking a smirk and nodding as he leaned in and kissed her forehead and squeezed her frame.

"It's okay. I understand," he said, resting his forehead against her own when he gazed down at her. There was nothing he wanted more than simply her at the moment and he would never admit that she was right but she was. After the events that they went through, acting on impulse would be a sure fire way to get one of them hurt. Or worse, killed.

"I'll see you in the morning? I can let your Dad know that

you'll want to meet with him. He was worried about you too," Chase said, his thumb running over the cut on her forehead before cracking a smile.

"No, no, stay," she said, glancing around the small apartment before looking back to him. "I just... we can't do this but you can stay here, with me. I don't want to be alone right now." If there was anything Cassidy hated, it was being weak, especially having to show that weakness in front of people that she cared about. But, after dealing with everything she experienced and learned, there was no way she felt comfortable being by herself.

"Yeah, no, I can stay here, that's—that's fine," he said, glancing around the room before rubbing the back of his head with his hand. "I'll just grab the co—"

"I'm not twelve, Chase. As long as you don't hog the bed or snore, you can sleep with me," she teased, pushing him from in front of her and exhaling, the euphoric shocks from their bond dwindling when they weren't so close to one another. She felt like she could breathe but she also wanted nothing more than to go back to his arms.

"Whatever you say, Cass," he laughed, tossing his hands into the air as to surrender, following after her into her room and quickly falling asleep.

Chapter 12

Cassidy was running, sprinting even, her heart exploding in her chest as she rounded the corner. She begged her feet to make her move even faster, the leftover adrenaline pumping through her chest egging her on to find her way out. A quick turn to the left found a large brick wall. Dead end. She screamed and pounded on it with her fists, the wall not moving a budge which prompted her to turn on her heel and try a different direction. Turning back the way she came, she took the hallway to her right and came to yet another crossroads. She felt a pull to her left and on instinct, she turned, pushing her body to its limits as it continued to carry her.

Another turn and she found another dead end. "Let me out!" she bellowed, her hair a disaster upon her head, sweat pouring from her brow. Her shirt was soaked around the neck and her boots were splattered with blood, although it was obvious that none of it was her own. The fact that she wasn't even trying to conjure her Origin terrified her but not enough to try. It was as if she were on autopilot and she were simply watching herself fall into a pit of destruction. "Help me! Anybody! Please!" she cried out, her voice breaking as she smacked the wall that was now in front of her. She couldn't hear anyone else's footsteps so she turned back towards the crossroads that she was pulled to go left before and went right. The hallways shifted and changed as she pushed on, changing even before she had the ability to make a decision. As the walls shifted, she could see someone off in the distance, a woman. It took her eyes a moment to realize who it was on the other side of the walls but once she did, her heart pounded even faster.

"Mom!" she screamed, her feet finding a way to move even faster through the maze that was growing harder and harder to climb through. The walls changed once more, Cassidy spotting her mother and someone else in front of her but she was far too away to see who it was.

"Mom, I'm coming! Come to me! Mom, can you hear me?!" she yelled, rounding yet another corner but the figure was gone once more, hidden behind the ever changing walls. "I'm coming! Mom, where are you?" she pleaded, her voice heavy as the energy started to leave her but she pressed on anyway. A step to the right and suddenly the wall to her left started to move once more. Cassidy anticipated the move and went to turn into it when the wall became a sludge like substance, enveloping Cassidy's frame like quick sand.

"No! Let me go!" she screamed, trying to free herself but struggling just made it worse. Before she knew it, her entire body was encased in a sand like substance, pulling her deeper and deeper into the maze.

"Mom! I can't—Mom, I need your help! Mom, please, save me!" Cassidy tried screaming one last time but by the time the words left her lips, the maze had consumed her and she was gone.

Cassidy cried out as she snapped up in bed, Chase

sprawled out on the other side away from her and she was thankful that she didn't manage to wake him. The bed sheets were soaked from sweat, Cassidy's heart eagerly throbbing in her chest at the nightmare. It was strange, seeing as she hadn't dreamt of her mother since she, supposedly, committed suicide over a year ago. Since becoming an Exodus member, she really hadn't thought of her at all until Caleb brought her up yesterday. She had a huge role in this life that Cassidy was now living and she felt guilty for everything. From what the League had told her, her mother died, basically, to protect her. Whether that was a fragment of the truth or not, Cassidy couldn't just let it be. She needed to know answers and rest would never come to her if she didn't figure it all out.

She pushed her feet out of the bed, grabbing up Chase's button down shirt and pulling it on over her bra and underwear, quietly sneaking out of the room and into the kitchen. A wave of her hand started the coffee pot, manipulating the electrical elements inside the machine to start brewing and she sat down at the kitchen island with a heavy sigh.

"No amount of coffee in the world would make me feel better right now," she mumbled to herself, rubbing her temples that were throbbing and pushing her hair out of her face. Today was the day that she would stand in front of the Chancellor, knowing what she knew on a grand scale. Of course, there was a lot that they would say is false—mainly all the things painting the Exodus in a bad light and she had promised herself that she would let the Chancellor air his side of the truth just as openly as she let Caleb.

Cassidy let Chase sleep, pulling on a pair of jeans and buttoning up Chase's shirt that she had stolen and tying the excess fabric at the base of her stomach. Her hair was brushed and curly around her shoulders and she left for the Chancellor's office before she told Chase goodbye.

The walk down to his office was the longest she'd ever experienced. Each step reminded her of her dream and she felt the pit in her stomach well up as she neared his office. She couldn't peg if she was worried because she was reminded of her dream or the fact that she was going to see her Dad and know that he was her Dad. It was so twisted, it was almost laughable to her. And, before she knew it, she was outside his office.

"I shouldn't be doing this alone," she said to herself with a quick laugh, raising her fist to knock before dropping it. "Nope, definitely should not do it alone," she mumbled, spinning on her heels to walk back to her room.

"Cassidy," the Chancellor's voice called out from his desk, the man going over papers at his desk. She instantly felt in trouble, stopping herself from moving away from the door. Her heart accelerated and she could feel the blood pooling in her cheeks almost instantly.

How could someone she barely knew cause such a reaction from just her name? At the end of the day, because of him, she had no idea who the man behind the desk was. To her, he was nothing but DNA. Her father died with her in that car.

Cassidy didn't go there to back off, though. She needed answers and he seemed to have them all wrapped up in a little bow. So, regardless of what she may have felt or how much she wanted to run, she needed to listen to him.

Her knuckles knocked on the mahogany, edging the door open just enough to cause it to creak and she locked eyes with the man sitting behind the desk. A few seconds ticked by and she finally pushed it open, leaning against the doorframe.

"Hey," she said softly, giving him a nod. "I didn't mean to interru- if you're busy, I mea- I can come back la—" She tried to get out but the Chancellor stopped her mid sentence with his wave to come sit down at the chair in front of him.

"Come in, come in. I expected you earlier, if I'm honest," he smiled, moving to close the door behind her before sitting back behind his desk, Cassidy slipping into the chair that he pointed to.

"I had a long night, needed some rest," she said, fiddling with her fingers as she tried to settle herself in the chair. The amount of anxiety welling up inside her was pretty par for the course for facing one's Dad, regardless of if you knew him or not.

"Of course. Chase said that he thought you'd appreciate meeting him instead of an entire welcoming committee. I would've met you when you got back but, I thought it best not to overwhelm you more than you already had been," the Chancellor reasoned, pulling the glasses from his face and pinching the bridge of his nose. "You seem to be generally unharmed, that's a plus, at least." He sighed as he looked his daughter over. For her to be sitting in front of him but have no idea who the man was, was heartwrenching. He'd watched her grow up for over twenty years but the past year, she was forced to forget who he was. She didn't remember him watching over her for entire childhood. Never would she remember what songs he would sing to put her to sleep. Every minute of every day was spent in service and protection of his daughter and now, she would never remember that feeling for the rest of her life. The daughter that he had raised no longer existed. He felt like he had to distance himself from the Cassidy that sat in front of him, otherwise he'd lose himself to the guilt of taking away the last thing that he created that was still absolutely pure.

"I appreciate it, I'm fine, really. I learned some things… that I'd like to clarify with you, for my mind, at least," she said, the both of them nodding at her comment. Of course she'd have questions.

"Well, I don't know what all they told you but yes, I'm your father," he said gently, leaning back in his chair to watch her reaction. He could see the frown form on her face, even if it was involuntary. "I know you're confused… why I went through the things that I went through to protect you, but, you need to know that I did it to protect you. I love you with every fiber of my being, Cassidy and I'd rather die than see anything happen to you," he said, closing the folder in front of him and clasping his hands together to listen to what she had questions about.

"But, why? Wouldn't it make more sense for you to protect me to keep me close? Why... why send me away when it sounds like I needed you the most?" Her voice broke, something she couldn't stop from happening, and she wiped away the tear that tried to roll down her cheek.

The Chancellor sighed, licking his lips and coughing for a moment before continuing. "Your mother was sick. She was unstable and using erradictly. She attacked another member of her Origin and when she broke the law, I was forced to exile her. It was only a few weeks later that the League killed her. They tried taking her, using her as a bargaining chip to get me to surrender but." He stopped, licking his bottom lip for a moment and thinking how to continue his sentence without losing it. "I loved your mother. She was the most exquisite human being I have ever met but, the Exodus exists above her, above me, above all of us. We're here to hold a balance, to protect those in this society and to protect us from those who would want us destroyed. So, when they took your mother, there was nothing I could do. It was only a matter of time till they killed her when she wasn't useful anymore." The Chancellor's gaze dropped, staring at his hands before taking in a deep breath and staring at Cassidy.

"They told me that you killed her," she said softly, chewing on the inside of her lip. Hearing the way that the Chancellor described his life with her mother broke her heart even more. How in the world could she believe what the League had fed her when it was clear that they were the ones who wanted to twist the truth.

The Chancellor instantly seemed hurt by her comment, offended that it was even a possibility. "I was wondering what they were saying to try and sway people to their cause. The League are a desperate sort of people. They have no family, no home, no sense of community and they'll hop on to anything to try and give them a semblance of that. They'll take a lie and spin it with some truth to make it just believable enough to get even the purest of heart to take it at face value. I hope... I hope you don't think I did that," he said, nearly begging his daughter to not assume he set up her mother's death.

"I—" she paused, running her hand over her face, her look obviously showing just how tired she actually was. "I don't know what to think anymore. My memories aren't even mine. You're my Dad. I made out with Chase last night and I was kidnapped for the better part of the day yesterday while some soul figure shit tried to give me the heebie jeebies," she blurted out, squishing her nose at how ridiculous she sounded but it got a laugh from the Chancellor and she laughed in unison. She leaned her head into her hand, propping her elbow upon the chair arm and stared at the man who was her father. Their dimples were similar. His eyes were hazel versus her blue ones. There was a dent in his nose from years of wearing eye glasses and his eyes had sunken into his face over time. They had similar facial structure, though, and the longer she stared at him, the more similarities she found.

"Well, your mother was really the one you turned to for boy advice but, I can try," he offered and Cassidy wrinkled her nose even more at his comment.

"I wouldn't even chat men with my other Dad, don't feel obliged—" she started before she frowned, resting her forehead on the inside of her palm. "I-I'm sorry, I didn't mean-he, he is all that I know. I don't- I don't know who you are," she said with a grimace. "Yet, at least. I'd like to get to know you," she offered, her lips turning up into a gentle smile. She couldn't pinpoint what was so great about him but she just felt relaxed talking to him. There was a sort of ease that she fell into without even knowing about it.

The Chancellor cracked a smile and nodded his head when she offered the last bit of her conversation. It meant the world to him that she was trying so hard to bridge the gap between the two of them. It was such a large gaping hole that they found themselves in that he would need her help to get over it.

"I agree. Getting to know the woman you are now, would be an honor, I assure you," he said with a grin. "Was there anything else that you wanted to go over with me while you're here?" he asked, arching a brow.

Cassidy, licked her lips and thought back to her time with the League, one particular part highlighting in her head. "I take it Mom didn't start the League, then, right?"

"Your mother, start the League? God, no. They hadn't come out and said who they were when she died but there were already a few others who were grouped together. When your mother was killed, it was a catalyst for this whole war we have going on. It's why the elders of each Origin asked to have you sent away. Your mother didn't want someone forcing you into triggering and I wanted to keep you from being used as a bargaining chip. You're too important." That seemed to be the argument that everyone had lately. Important. The key. The person that everyone wanted. But, why? To her, she was still so simple. Powerful, yes but nothing more than anyone else.

"Why? Why do so many people think that I'm this person to fulfill the prophecy or whatever," she said, completely disinterested in hearing about the prophecy any more than what the Chancellor had left to say.

"Because your mother, a Chi, said that the prophecy was to be fulfilled by someone close to me. Now, many thought that it would be her. Some think that it'll be Bryan, some think it'll be you and some think that your mother was just plain wrong but I know your mom. And she was hardly ever wrong," he said with a shrug. The facts were the facts. Half of the Exodus didn't even put much faith in the ideal of the prophecy but there were some, like the Chancellor who thought it had merit.

"Who's Bryan?" Cassidy questioned, bypassing everything

about the prophecy. She needed to know why this person was close to her father.

"You might have seen him when you were with the the League. He was a Delta when he was with the Exodus but, he's my nephew, your cousin. He was raised in my Origin from a baby. His mother, my sister, died in childbirth and so did he. An Omicron revived him in time to not only save his life but to trigger him as well." Bryan was a few years older than Cassidy but she didn't remember anything about him.

"The only one I saw at the League was Caleb, a Sigma. They held me in a channeling room and then when he let me out, I walked out of the door and was somehow brought back to my old house that I had back in town. I didn't see anyone else," she said with a shrug. It was clear that Cassidy was growing disinterested in reliving the lies that she had been told while she was held captive. The Chancellor was right. They took a truth that they knew would get her interest piqued and added in their own flair. If they told her a nugget of truth, she would be hook line and sinker for their team. It truly was ridiculous.

The Chancellor thought that it was odd the League kept her from so many people. Capturing her was one thing but to keep her deprived of all the people who could turn her against the Exodus was a strange tactic.

"Well... it doesn't matter anymore. You're here, you're safe and we're going to keep you safe. That is what matters now." The Chancellor reached out and grabbed Cassidy's hands, thumbing over the back of her knuckles and giving them a squeeze. She managed to get a genuine smile to grace her lips for a moment before squeezing them back and slinking her hands away.

"It's nice to be back," she whispered with a nod, pushing herself out of the chair and adjusting her shirt.

The Chancellor grabbed his glasses and placed them back on his head with a chuckle. "And maybe next time, don't come to meet with your father in your boyfriend's shirt," he said teasingly, giving her the best fatherly glare he could muster. Cassidy turned bright red but rolled her eyes and shrugged her shoulders.

"What? It fit and I make this look better than he does. Besides, we're not anything," she said nonchalantly, making it to the door and moving to exit before stopping herself. "I'm sorry I don't remember you. But, I promise, we'll make better memories," she said gently, flashing a smile before walking out.

"That we will," the Chancellor said with a nod after she walked away, going back to the work in front of him.

Chapter 13

Regardless of what truths she was presented with, they were incredibly overwhelming for Cassidy to process. The entire framework of the life that she understood was called into question. She just wanted to know what of her current memories were still the same as her original but the only person that would know that was gone forever.

Her fingers grasped her phone out of her back pocket, fiddling through the menus and landing on Chase's name, trying to think of a witty comment to make. Herr grin spread across her face, chewing on the inside of her lip as she typed, erased, typed some more and erased again. It'd be simpler to contact him via her bond but this was more... normal. And, while she was far from normal, there were certain aspects of her life that she wanted to keep magic out of.

As she compiled another text, ready to send and turning to head back to her room, she heard the yelling ripple down the corridor she was walking down. Her heart leapt at the sound, more than one voice booming in the middle of the room and the sound of a scuffle. Something was going down and Cassidy couldn't help but follow the sounds to the source. Whether it was curiousity or her sudden hero nature, she felt like she could help.

"You spineless rat!" an Omicron yelled at a man who was kneeled on the ground. The room was confusing when she entered. One man laid injured on the ground, bleeding from a wound to his abdomen. Cassidy recognized that the man who was injured was a Chi, Garrett, that was on security detail the first week she was at the Exodus. The Omicron was next to him, the blue igniting across his hands over the wound and trying desperately to stop the blood flow. The man who the Omicron was talking to was another Chi, a knife with blood dripping from it in his hands. Cassidy wasn't the only one who had followed the sounds of the argument, several others including the Chi elder, Ezekiel, finding the scene in front of him.

"What happened?" Ezekiel demanded. His voice was terrifyingly loud. She didn't know if it was because he was a Chi and he just had a charismatic charm about him or not but she felt compelled to spill everything that was in her mind at the moment to him. It actually took every fiber of her being to hold her tongue when he spoke.

"Jon was trying to leave the north wing defenseless. He-He was trying to give the League an easier entry point, sir," Garrett managed to get out as he was being worked on. The blue Omicron magic pulsed over his skin, trying desperately to save him and it was starting to work after a few moments ticked by. Ezekiel's gaze switched from the injured man of his Origin to the accused, watching as his hands were violently shaking. It was clear that the man was on withdrawals from something, whether he had stopped using magic or the League tortured him long enough to get him to flip sides, he was willing to kill to further their means.

"Stand, Jon!" Ezekiel barked out, Jon rising to his feet and dropping the knife to the ground and keeping his eyes lowered. There was no way that he could met Ezekiel's gaze in the state that he was in. Cassidy watched as the scene unfolded, terrified to ever become like Jon, terrified that the League would do whatever they deemed necessary to achieve their means. They were ready to do anything to bring the Exodus down.

"Not only did you harm a fellow Exodus member, you attacked another person within your Origin and tried to weaken our defenses. You have dishonored the Chi Origin and are hereby exiled. So say I, so shall it be." Ezekiel's voice filled the room in deafening silence, his arm grasping Jon's and the red magic that flowed between them was brighter than Cassidy had ever seen before. The pulse grew brighter until a loud and distinct pop echoed from Jon's body, his blood curdling scream ripping from his chest as he dropped to his knees. Never before had Cassidy watched as someone's connection to their Origin was stripped from them but watching it for the first time was enough to make her never want to see it again. The feeling to hurl stirred in her stomach, unable to hold it back as she bent at the waist and lost it. No one in the room even batted at eye at her getting sick. Perhaps they were used to such a reaction. She couldn't understand how everyone else was so calm as she listened to the screams of Jon writhing in pain. The color had drained from his face by the time she cleaned off her lips. The man looked like a fraction of the person he was not even five minutes before. She had heard stories of how hard magic addiction hit a person but to see someone have it completely stripped from their body, from their soul, it affected Cassidy in a way that she wasn't sure she would ever recover from.

"If I ever see you again, this pain will be laughable to what will happen to you. You have disgraced yourself for a lifetime, guards will escort you to the edge of the barrier and you are banished, forever," Ezekiel said, grabbing Jon up and tossing him towards the door where guards met him, dragging him away as his screams continued to echo against the walls. Cassidy wiped away the tears from her face, her heart nearly exploding out her chest once the action settled. She let her eyes settle on the blood on the floor, gazing at the knife that Jon had used to break the trust of his Origin and she was flabbergasted that one act, no matter how big or how small, pushed the Elder to exile him immediately. There was no trial, no jury of his peers; the Elder was jury, judge and executioner.

The only thing that managed to pull her from her daze was Chase entering the room, looking from his Elder to the two on the ground to finding Cassidy standing there, chest still heaving and the color drained from her face.

"Cass," he said, snapping her out of thoughts long enough to get her to raise her eyes to him, the pain evident on her face. His face dropped with hers, reaching out and squeezing her hand with a heavy sigh. "It's okay," he whispered, closing the space between them. He could tell how directly affected she was at watching what she saw, hearing the screams like she did. Maybe she wasn't as strong as he thought she was.

"No," she laughed derisively, shaking her head, "it's far from okay!" Her voice sounded broken but she swallowed hard, trying to push through her emotions. "We were attacked," she said, flatly, gazing from the knife on the floor to the healed Chi who was moving to his feet to the Elder. "Th- I could see it in Jon. I know what he was feeling," she swallowed hard, clearing her throat and wiping her mouth off with the back of her hand. "The League... they broke him until he had no other option," she defended, knowing that her take on the story that unfolded was different than most. Jon seemed desperate to save himself from the pain that he had experienced with the League. Cassidy had only experienced a fraction of that agony but she knew their tactics. She knew that they were depriving him just like they did her but probably to an indescribable extent.

"He had a responsibility to protect us all and to protect his

Origin and he chose to attack it. Plain and simple," Ezekiel said, dismissing Cassidy's comment entirely.

"No. No one makes that choice because they want to. Did you not hear his screams? He had no other option. The League... They're far more craftier than all of you give them credit for. They tell you a truth but pervert it with disgusting lies. They make the best thing seem tainted and they do it all while making you feel like you're in control. Well, they're controlling the narrative and it's time we stop taking the defensive. We need an offense. The only way to protect our people, to protect what we've grown here... to stop this war before it ever can get off the ground is to know our enemy. We need someone on the inside," Cassidy spoke and as the words left her mouth, her voice grew stronger. It was evident that she felt passionate about what she was saying. It didn't matter that her memory only spanned the past few months inside the Exodus. Her father was Chancellor, her mother was being painted as a traitor and had someone stuck up for the origins before she ever got sick, she might not have traveled down that path. Someone could've saved her. Cassidy couldn't just stand there and watch as someone else lost their mother, their father, their friend.

"And what, you think you're that person? No, never," Chase said with a laugh, shaking his head and Cassidy never looked more serious in her life.

"Why? They've already tried to recruit me. Who else has a better chance of working them? They need me more than we need them. And, I can do this! Look at me and tell me I'm wrong," she said, squeezing his hand as she pitched her case, trying desperately to have him see her potential.

"You're wrong!" he said, not even contemplating it. "It's not safe. Your father would never put you in harms way again and you're too much of an asset to risk out there. If they found out, they'd have you killed and then where would we be? We wouldn't have you anymore." Chase couldn't stop the words from leaving his lips but they were on the table nonetheless. Whether he would admit it or not, he cared for the woman who was volunteering to risk her life for a cause that she barely knew. "If anything, it should be me in there. I'm a Chi, I can use my abilities to my advantage. If I get caught? A wave of the hand can fix that," he said, straightening his jacket.

"You're practically the Counsellor's right hand. You defecting wouldn't make the least bit of sense and they wouldn't feel apt to spill their beans to you because you're a Chi. Your Origin leads you to be untrustworthy, despite that face of yours. I'm an Epsilon. I can show vulnerability. Besides, I'm still new. I'm still a baby in their eyes. I am a better bait and you damn well know it."

"The decision isn't either of yours to make. If we're going to risk anyone, it has to be a unanimous decision. All five Elders and the Chancellor will have to agree to putting you in a position where you could die. Or be tortured. Or be pushed to your breaking point. You could fail, you have to know that before going in. Being a double agent wanes on you after a while. This isn't something that you can enter in lightly, Miss Hawkins." Ezekiel closed the space between them and watched as he spoke to Cassidy, trying to gauge her heart. For someone so new to the fold to feel so strongly about a cause was surprising but after all she had experienced, it wasn't far fetched.

"You let me know when I get the go," she said, standing her ground and not backing away from him, despite her utter terror of him. He was such a large man who commanded a respect that oozed from his skin that she only wished that she would be in the same shoes one day. Ezekiel's firm glare let way for a bit of a smirk, nodding to her and then looking to Chase. "We'll make our decision by day's end," he said, looking disapprovingly at Chase for his utter lack of confidence in Cassidy's ability to hold herself up. It wasn't that Chase didn't think she could do the job, he was fearful that she'd end up like Sebastian, eventually. He knew all too well what the League could do with magic and he knew that Cassidy would rather die than admit to her faults and weaknesses.

Ezekiel walked off, helping Garrett and the Omicron to the infirmary to ensure their safety in the fight and to alert the other Elders and the Chancellor of the undertaking that Cassidy had volunteered for. When the others had left, Chase stared Cassidy down, his face already displaying his utmost distaste for what she had gotten herself into.

"You're ridiculous," he complained, turning away from the fight that he knew was about to start and trying to walk out of the room.

"I'm-what are you saying? Are you saying that what I said didn't make every bit of sense to you? Because, I don't see any fail in my logic. The League isn't going to trust that you've suddenly seen the error of your ways and I'm the perfect person to put in such a position." Cassidy quickly caught up after him, Chase leading them down the hallways back to her room.

"But that's just it! There's a reason you're perfect for this job!" Chase spat out, walking faster as if he was trying to get away from her.

"No... you're-you don't trust me," she said, hurt by the words that left her lips as she stopped walking next to him. "You actually think... how could you?" she demanded, standing firm in the hallway, unwilling to just let the conversation go.

"Cassidy," he said, exhaustion rolling from his body. "That's not what I meant. You're still reeling from the other night, you don't know what's even going on in your actual life and now you're volunteering to be a double agent?! Don't you see how bad that could go? You... they're smart. Far smarter than I give them credit and you don't know them like I know them. They will sink their claws into you and make you believe we're the bad guys and I can't just let you abandon everything that we've grown here to play some heroic quest." Cassidy listened to him practically beg for her not to go and before she knew it, she closed the space between them and pulled his frame to her, eagerly lifting her lips to his own. Her fingers snaked through the strands of his hair, pulling him closer to her lips, tugging on his bottom lip with her teeth before releasing him, making sure to lock her eyes with his.

"I'm perfect for this because I have something no one else has. You. You ground me here, in the home that I've made here. You have a bond with me that keeps me from forgetting what I'm growing here. My father is here, you're here, I'm not going anywhere, I promise you. I'm protecting what I've made. I'm fighting for this," she whispered, resting her frame against his as he held her to him. He blinked a few times before smirking and shaking his head.

"You're going to be the death of me, you know?" he teased, leaning down for one more kiss before letting her go and leading her back to her room. Cassidy laughed, shoving him slightly as they walked. It was so easy with him that she found it terrifying her, almost more than going into the League. She'd never felt this way about anyone else, ever. She couldn't quantify it with a word just yet but she felt like she was headed down that path. And, if there was anything more terrifying than making oneself bait, it was the possibility of falling in love.

Chapter 14

Minutes felt like days once the meeting was called between the Elders. It wasn't a publicized meeting, no one else other than the ones that were in the room and the Elders knew what Cassidy had proposed to do. It was crazy, if she were honest. Complete madness but Cassidy wouldn't be herself if she didn't fight for what she believed in. She knew that her father would be the one to approve the entire stunt and if she didn't have him on board, it would never fly.

"I just wish they would give me an update already," she mumbled, playing with the food in front of her on the plate, forking some of the spaghetti and then unspinning it, her fork scraping against the porcelain plate.

"I'm telling you to calm down," Chase said with a laugh, cleaning up the plate that he had already finished, a knock on the door distracting the two of them before he was able to continue. "See, maybe your worry will be eased," he said, walking to the door. Quickly answering it, Olivia was on the other side and Chase was honestly relieved that it wasn't her father. At least he had a bit more time with her before she left for possible slaughter.

"Oh, hello," she said, surprised at Chase answering the door and peering over his shoulder to look at Cassidy, wiggling her eyebrows when Chase looked away from her. Cassidy rolled her eyes, thankful to get up from the food that she was unable to eat and greeting her at the door.

"Sight for sore eyes," she teased, pushing Chase out of the way and letting her into her apartment, welcoming her to a seat and gesturing to the drinks in the fridge if she chose to partake. "Need something?" She asked, arching a brow as she sat back at the kitchen island and Olivia shook her head.

"No, I thought we'd get some much needed training time in but it looks like I've kinda interrupted something else," she teased and Chase laughed, moving to grab his jacket and slinging it over his shoulders before moving back to Cassidy's side.

"I'll let you know when I know, alright?" he said, leaning down and pressing his lips firmly against hers, taking her off guard in front of someone else. There was a difference between being close in private and publicly showing affection for one another. Not that she was complaining by any means, it just wasn't something she was anticipating. Olivia tried to hide her grin behind her hand as she looked away, giving the apparent couple a few moments by themselves before Chase excused himself, leaving the women by themselves.

"Well, seems like you've been doing just fine," Olivia teased, waggling her eyebrows which caused Cassidy to blush and shake her head again, clearing off her plate and putting it in the sink.

"It's kinda been pretty sudden but... good, I think. We'll see, I guess, right?" she said, both as an assumption and as a question.

"Chase isn't one for connections, generally, so to see him

close to someone is a nice change. He's been pretty distant since he lost his sister Holly and his brother Sebastian," she said with a shrug, pulling a pillow to her chest and hugging it close as she watched Cassidy's reaction.

"Sebastian? That's the name of his brother?" she asked, her interest piqued nearly instantly. It wasn't that the name wasn't uncommon but for her to meet a Sebastian the same night she was kidnapped by the League, that couldn't be coincidence.

"Yeah, really twisted history between them too. Rumors were that Sebastian lost his shit to his Origin, killed his sister in a forced trigger gone wrong and defected to the League nearly instantly. Did you not meet him when they had you there?" Olivia questioned and Cassidy shook her head, grabbing two bottles of water and heading to the couch.

"Nah, they kept me in a pretty isolated area. Probably for the best, I guess," she said with a shrug, instantly wondering why Chase hadn't let her in on that bit of information. If his brother was still inside the League, there was always the possibility that her inside job could not only solve the issue between the two groups but she could try and mend the bad blood between the two of them too. Chase had lost so much to this war already and it hadn't even truly started yet. If Cassidy could bring him some solace, she would definitely try.

"I'm glad you're safe, you know. We were all so worried about you," Olivia said, cracking a smile and reaching out to squeeze her hand. "We tried to find you but wherever they had you wasn't accessible to us." Her smile dropped to a frown. "All that matters is that you're safe," she said, taking a quick drink of water. Cassidy managed a smile and nodded, playing with the label of her beer nervously.

"Yeah, I agree. All of us safe and sound, healthy and thriving, that's all that matters," she said gently, taking a quick sip of her water as Olivia noticed her demeanor.

"Are you alright? We haven't really had a chance to talk since you got back. I'm sorry that I didn't get to come down here sooner," she said, shaking her head but Cassidy cut her off before she could continue.

"No—no need to be sorry. I had a lot to do when I got back. Spent some time trying to catch up with my Dad, channeled in the Epsilon room to feel more at ease, don't feel bad." She knew that she had to stay quiet about her possible new task that the elders were deciding on but she felt like Olivia deserved to know something.

"How is everyone? I'm sure everyone has heard about what happened," Cassidy asked, chewing on her lip, adjusting her weight on the couch.

"We're fine. Worried, obviously, but, we're just glad you're whole. And with us. It's devastating for everyone to lose a member and you, we just were worried," Olivia said, pushing herself from the couch and holding her hand out to her, grinning. "Why don't you come out with a few of us? We'll promise to return you with every hair still in place on your head and it'd do you some good." She grinned, half dancing in front of her which garnered a laugh out of Cassidy. As much as a night out sounded like a great plan, she knew that the elders could come back to a decision at any time and she needed to be ready.

"While every part of that sounds like a good idea, I don't think I'm ready just yet. Maybe... soon? I'll take a rain check and when I'm feeling up for it, we'll party until I'm too drunk to think straight, deal?" She grinned, but Olivia seemed slightly sad that she didn't take her up on her offer.

Olivia nodded, accepting the rain check. "You got it. Keep me informed on the Chase front, alright? Fill me in on the juicy details when you have some," Olivia giggled, waving as she left Cassidy's apartment and left her all by herself.

The ten minute conversation sealed the deal even more than this endeavor, should it happen, was worth any negative she should face. Cassidy could and would do this better than anyone else to ensure that Olivia and the others could continue to enjoy their lives like they had for years.

Chapter 15

*Y*our mother would be proud of your bravery," the Chancellor mused, watching as his daughter paced inside the Epsilon channeling room, careful to stay outside the edges of the room. It was surprisingly quiet and empty, minus the two of them. The Chancellor even managed to convince Chase to give them some time together before she left. It *had* only been a few hours since the elders agreed to let Cassidy infiltrate the League. Many had their doubts but the Chancellor trusted his daughter.

"Yeah, I feel pretty much terrified right now," she muttered, rubbing her arms to warm them up as she tried to settle her nerves. The purpose of even sitting in the room was to calm her heart rate and restore her strength. There was no telling what the League would do when they found her. They could believe her, torture her, even kill her if they wanted to. The possibilities were endless.

"That's to be expected," the Chancellor added, leaning

against the doorframe and crossing his arms over his chest. "But, we don't have much time... " he added and Cassidy quickly nodded her head.

"Yeah, yeah, I know," she said reluctantly, exiting the room and rubbing her sweaty palms against the thighs of her jeans. Anticipation rolled over her frame and waves and it took everything in her essence to attempt to control it.

"We wouldn't have said yes if we didn't think you could do this. Remember the woman who requested this assignment in the first place. You are the best person for the job," he said, wrapping his arms around her and kissing the top of her head. "I love you," he added, rubbing her back affectionately and instead of pushing him away, Cassidy wrapped her arms around him and accepted his comments to her. It was strange, at first, but she soon shook away the concern and embraced the man in front of her as what he was. Her father.

"I wanna make you proud, too. You gave up so much to protect me, it's time I paid that debt back," she said, pulling back to look up at him. "I can do this. And, Chase will be the first one to know if something has gone wrong," she said with a nod, glancing to Chase who was walking down the hallway towards them.

"Speak of the devil," the Chancellor teased, releasing his daughter and looking to Chase, giving him a respectful nod.

"I'm not the Devil. I'm sure he'd be very upset to hear you say that. I know I've heard some Sigmas contacting him recently," Chase teased with a wink, instinctively returning to Cassidy's side with a heavy sigh. He knew that he'd have to let her go but he hated he had grown so attached in the first place.

"Take care of my daughter, Mr. Williams, or I promise I'll be worse than what the devil could deliver," the Chancellor said without cracking a smile or a joke, nodding to them both before exiting.

"Isn't he just peachy," he said with a laugh before turning to Cassidy. "You ready?" he asked, brushing back a few strands of hair as she nodded.

"As ready as I'll ever be, I guess. If I fiddle any longer, I'm bound to change my mind," she laughed, reaching out to touch him. She knew how hard the next however long would be for her. Accepting that she was going to have to play the role that was laid out before her was one thing but knowing what she was going to be giving up in the meantime was what was sickening her.

"I won't be far away," he whispered, thumbing over her cheek as the two stood, saying their goodbyes for God knew how long. "And, if things get bad, I'm only a thought away." Chase leaned down, pressing his lips to hers with a heavy sigh, angry at himself for waiting so long to try his feelings at something with Cassidy.

"I know, I'll be fine, I've had a pretty good teacher," she teased, resting her head on his chest and closing her eyes, trying anything to remember the moment before everything changed. It wouldn't be easy and Cassidy understood that. But, she'd come to realize how different understanding a hardship was versus experiencing one. "Like you said, you're barely a thought away. We'll meet when we can to debrief to the elders, I'll get what we need to bring the League down without any more bloodshed and then we can go on being... us," she said, lifting her head and pulling away with a nod. "Promise," she said, holding out and wiggling her pinkie to him with a girlish laughter, Chase rolling his eyes as he clasped his finger around her own.

"Alright, alright, off you go," he said, pushing her towards the front barrier of the Exodus defenses. She couldn't be delivered to where she was going, she'd have to find a way to get there on her own means. The minute she walked out of the safety of the Exodus, she was truly on her own and up to her own devices.

"I'll be back before you know it," she said, squeezing his hand before meeting the cab on the road out front. Ever since she died, cars were not something that she was comfortable in controlling so when she was face with a normal way to get back home, she opted for the personal driver.

Her skin sunk against the thick black leather of the seat, the smell of sweat and poor decisions wafting through the air. It tookay everything within her to not roll the window down while sitting in the back seat. Her eyes lifted to meet the gaze of the driver and her mind filled with questions. Did he drive people from the Exodus often and if he did, had he seen her before? Did Chase's father go as far as to erase her old life from everyone who had met her? Her mind wandered as her eyes watched the world pass by, the car moving faster as it hit the open road. Bushes became blurs, stars turned into blinking entities long forgotten and as the ride grew longer, her eyelids became heavier. With each bump and lift in the road, she felt herself drifting deeper.

It wasn't long before she was asleep, her chest content with rising and falling with the breaths that left her. Her dreams grew as she fell deeper into sleep and before she knew it, she was dreaming something close to reality.

She was perched at the kitchen island of her apartment, eating a bowl of cereal and playing with a random newspaper. Each time she went to read it, the words would jumble and she soon realized that she wasn't meant to be focusing on the words but the environment that she was in.

"Cassy, did you borrow my sweater? The blue one with the white stitching?" Elizabeth called from one of the rooms down the hall. The layout was almost identical to her current apartment but with minor differences, the largest one being a room off to the left that was far bigger than her own room. She could see photos of herself, the family, her father and her mother—her actual parents—and before she could take in anymore of the scenery, Elizabeth was standing in front of her. The woman was just as tall as Cassidy, her hair a bit lighter in a gray sort of tone and her face had aged well despite the crows feet spreading at the corners of her eyes. Her lips were done in a mauve color and the woman was quite put together except for the missing sweater that she was questioning.

"Mom?" Cassidy asked, swallowing back whatever emotions were coming to the surface. "Mo- what, what are you doing here? How are you here?"

"How am I here- What do you mean?" she asked, brushing back the edge of Cassidy's hair with a laugh. "I live here and you and Chase are bound to be getting the apartment on another floor here soon so soon I'll be asking you why you're here," she teased, bopping her on the nose with a grin.

"How do you know about Chase?" she mumbled, glancing around the room and noticing that the photos of her were also photos of her and Chase peppered about the room. Her hand went to her forehead, rubbing it with a groan. What was going on?

"Sweetheart, what has gotten into you? You and Chase have been together for a few years now, we're surprised it took you this long to move in," she teased, trying to figure out why her daughter was so upset. It was strange for Cassidy as she listened to her mother. It was as if her mind was trying to show her this perfect life that she could've had had the League not gotten in the way. She'd be sharing clothes with her mom, moving in with Chase, remembering what her father was like to her. Her life would be perfect.

"Right, I'm sorry, my head just hurts. Guess it made me forget for a minute," she said with a shrug, gazing up at her mother. It was crazy to see their resemblances and Cassidy took her dream as a minute to study every single feature of her mother's face. There was so much she'd forgotten over the course of the year that she was desperate to instil them in her mind now.

"Just make sure you're careful. Don't want you running yourself thin. Protect yourself first, then others," her mother cautioned, staring at her daughter before the seriousness melted away and Cassidy perked up, arching a brow at her statement. She couldn't figure out why her mother said those specific words and as her mind started thinking on it, she started to drift away from her.

"Mom?" she asked, the maze walls started moving around her once more, like they did the last time she dreamt of her mother. Before she could fight any longer, the taxi driver was calling her ma'am, waking her as best he could as they sat outside the childhood home that she had no true connection anymore.

"I'm sorry," Cassidy said with a sigh, grabbing up her bag and slipping the cab driver the cash that she owed him and walking up to the door.

"Home sweet home," she sighed. The frame of the house in front of her was so familiar that her body automatically started to calm down. She hated that her memories betrayed the way she wanted to enter the building. Double agent or not, this truly wasn't the home that she grew up in. She really didn't sneak out of the top window to meet boys or scrape her knee on the front steps. Every single memory that was floating around in her head was fake. Cassidy understood that there was a purpose, much like there was a purpose around everything in life, but to pervert her mind in such a way so that she couldn't trust what she remembered... it was rough. But, a part of life, nonetheless.

Cassidy took one last shaky breath before walking into the house, turning on the lights and instinctively locking the door behind her. There wasn't a true plan in seeking the League out. Everyone knew that they were wanting to get their nails into Cassidy so they thought the easiest way to lure them in would be to do nothing. Simply existing outside of the walls of the Exodus was enough to ensure they'd visit her. For now, she'd simply have to wait.

She dropped her bag off at the door, slipping out of her shoes and walked into her kitchen, grabbing up a bottle of merlot and pouring herself a rather large glass of wine. If she were going to wait, alone, she was going to have an enjoyable wait.

And, apparently she wasn't going to have to wait long.

Before the glass even hit her lips, a knock at the door echoed through the house. It seemed louder than it used to since the entire house was eerily silent. Ruca was still at her apartment back in the Exodus and the only real sounds inside the house was the heat slowly rumbling to life. Cassidy's heart started to accelerate, allowing herself to take the quick sip of wine before walking towards the door. The only luxury she had if it was another Origin member was the fact that they couldn't enter without her express permission. It was one Origin failsafe that she was suddenly excited existed.

She stood at the door, her hand outreached to yank it open and she waited. A few deep breaths, managing to settle her heart rate and once she pulled it open, she saw someone she didn't necessarily expect to be there. If anything, she expected Caleb or Geneva to be the one to greet her.

"Didn't think you'd answer," Sebastian said with a grin, leaning against the front porch pillar near the front door. He had jeans on, a gray t-shirt and a jacket over that. His hair was similar to Chase's, long enough to flow in the wind but not past his ears. Actually, the longer she looked at his face, the more she could notice the similarities between the two of them. It was strange that she never put two and two together before, surprisingly. She could tell, however, that through his looks, which were just as charming as Chase's, that he was dealing with addiction issues. His eyes were slightly sunken into his face. It looked like it'd been weeks since he had a decent night sleep. Suddenly the emotions that she felt when she watched Jon become stripped of his connection to the Exodus rolled over her. His screams filled her ears and it took everything inside of her to push through the emotions and crack a smile accompanied by a laugh. She had an appearance to keep up.

"Didn't think I'd be followed home," she said with a shrug, crossing her arms over her chest as she continued to make note of his appearance. "Also didn't think for you to be some hidden League member but, what do you really know these days," she added, the disdain strong enough to cause Sebastian to laugh. The man put his arms up in the air, whistling softly.

"And she comes out swinging! Not even five seconds into a conversation. I think I owe Caleb some money for that one. I gave you at least a minute before you either attacked or said something snarky. Guess he got to know you a bit better than I did the last time we met." Sebastian shoved his hands in his jeans pockets, watching Cassidy size him up which intrigued him more than her snark. That was an admirable quality.

"Last time we met, all I found out was that you were lying the entire time," she said, narrowing her eyes for a moment, leaning against the edge of the door.

"I like to think that it's all about omitting the truth. You didn't ask, I didn't say," he said, rather nonchalantly. "Now, I came here to chat and you're being quite rude keeping me outside... " He glanced at the door, knowing the invisible barrier that was preventing him from coming inside.

"You lied. You knew who I was the minute you saw me. You were there for a reason. You helped kidnap me," she said bluntly, standing up just a bit straighter than moments before. "And you've lost your mind if you think that I'm going to give up the only sanctuary that I have on this Earth. A place that can be completely and utterly all mine, forever," Her hand ran up the doorframe as she realized how thankful she was for the home she was standing in. Fake memories or not, no triggered member from either side could get inside that home, other than Chase. That was the biggest mode of protection she could ever ask for.

"I was simply following orders, trying to get to know you outside of this... whatever this whole mess is." Sebastian sounded exhausted, despite his best efforts. He tried putting up a strong front and to anyone else, he probably could master it but Cassidy was eerily perceptive. Perhaps it was her bond to Chase and knowing that the same blood that flowed through him, flowed through Sebastian.

"It's war, and, it doesn't look like either one of us will manage to win it, if I'm being honest," she said with a heavy sigh, running her hand over her face. She had to figure out a way to pitch her switching sides.

"Look, if we're gonna chat and I'm not coming in, at least come out. Promise, I'll keep my hands to myself," he said, putting his hands up once again and flipping them back and forth as if to prove that nothing was up his sleeves, at least literally. Cassidy continued to size him up, watching, wishing more than ever that she could just read his mind and figure out what he was thinking. Was he really just there because he knew she was there? Was he there to kidnap her again? There were so many things running through her head that before she knew it, she was crossing the threshold of her door. She was out in the open which caused her pulse to vibrate even faster. Each throb of her heart pounded faster against her ribcage, her nerves pooling sweat in her palms.

"See? Better, yeah?" Sebastian said, moving to sit on the steps leading up to her door, patting the wood next to him for her to sit. Cassidy rolled her eyes but begrudgingly followed after him.

"If you try anything..." she trailed off, green igniting across her hands, the magic dancing from finger to finger, eager to be put to work. Sebastian stared at the color cascading about and wished for a moment that he could do the same. He knew the dangers and temptation to using and promised himself that he'd avoid it at all costs. Cold turkey was a luxury he couldn't afford but tapered use was better than nothing.

"Hey, have I threatened you yet? I'm here not for fighting. I'm here because we weren't expecting you to be allowed out of the Exodus, let alone come back here, alone. So, we assumed that there was a reason for that. I drew the short straw," he teased, watching as the woman took the seat next to him, dispersing the green from her hand and wrapping her arms around her waist.

"I saw- there was a man, Jon. He- uh- was trying to weaken their defenses. I had just left my dad's office and saw the attack. And then I watched as they stripped him of his connection to the Exodus. The screams..." She swallowed hard, reaching up and brushing the water from the edges of her eyes, glancing over to him. "Every time I close my eyes, I can hear it. That popping noise, everything just goes on replay in my head. They didn't even have him plead his defense. It all happened so fast and I just don't think." She paused, swallowing back her emotions, whether they were real or not. "I don't think I can support a cause that acts so swiftly. His entire world was uprooted without even a bat of an eye." Cassidy gazed back out to the street, watching as the trees leaned too and fro through the wind.

"I know what that's like. It causes this gaping hole that nothing can fill. Even being apart of the League only tries to fill it. You don't realize what you sign up for when you take that oath at the choosing ceremony. Your Origin bonds to every aspect of your body but when the Exodus decides to exile you, they rip a wound into every crevice possible. I still remember every second, every flicker of pain that happened when Ezekiel separated me from Chi. It was unbearable for months." Sebastian's voice was soft and surprisingly open but he quickly cleared his throat, watching her while she watched the road.

"So, have you thought about our offer? Joining us?" Sebastian arched a brow at the woman and she shrugged.

"I'm not sure what I want right now. But, I don't think I can decide without knowing what there is to know. I just... needed to get out of there. To see what was worth having my soul ripped apart. And, I don't know if the League gives a trial period or a ninety day supply or whatever but, if you do, I'd like to test it out." Cassidy chewed on the inside of her lip, her heart trying to pound faster at the lies she was spewing, regardless of how true they started to sound. Sebastian was a Chi and just because he wasn't on board with using his Origin, that didn't mean that others thought the same way. If she could control her nervousness now, she'd have it mastered before long.

Sebastian stared at the woman. He could see her fidgeting, watched as the pulse on her neck escalated with each word. He couldn't truly see if it was accelerating out of terror, lying or just plain nerves. Most would assume a little of both and that was what Sebastian was going with. How could someone who seemed so affected by what happened knowingly stay within the walls of the Exodus. He commended her effort to get out as soon as she was feasibly able to.

"I can let Geneva know that that is what you're interested in doing. Whether or not that happens will be her call. Depending on her mood, of course. You Epsilons are known to have emotions much like the elements. Unpredictable," he teased with a wink, running his thumb over his hand, changing his gaze from her to the road once more. "You'll like it here, if you wanna know my opinion. I know you feel or felt at home with the Exodus. I did too. So did Chase which I'm sure you know. He's all over you," he said, looking back to her as she blushed, her tongue running over her bottom lip and he watched as she arched her brow at him.

"How do you know that?" she said with a laugh, looking at her clothes.

"I'm magic, remember? Even without using, I can tell that you're surrounded in my Chi Origin. And, while it's not me using at the moment, it must be a remnant of someone else. Seeing as he is joined to you, I just put two and two together," he said and shrugged. "If you choose us, that'll have to end, you know? Other than the fact that star crossed lovers are a big no-no, we can't have you joined to an Exodus member. If Geneva approves the trial period, that'll be the first thing to go once you're officially one of us." Sebastian was trying to break the news to her earlier rather than later but he even wanted to break it nearly instantly. It was a tricky process but it was possible. And, personally, he hated the idea of being forcibly attached to another person just because they brought you back to life. In his mind, someone should be able to decide if they want to join to someone. But, magic was a tricky little game. More often than not, it did things that you didn't want it to but that you needed it to.

"I assumed so. It's why I need to think so hard on this decision. I don't expect open arms. I don't expect sunflowers and daisies but... I need to know I'm making the right choice before I make it. I need to know that we can end this war without any more bloodshed and with the good of the people at the forefront. I need to know that I can do some good," she said, her voice growing more genuine as she spoke, staring at her hands. The most she saw so far with magic was the ugly or the manipulative that could be done with it. She wanted to see the life changing aspects.

"I can't promise we're all sunshine and rainbows but we're the good guys. We may not show it all the time. We may be a bit unorthodox in our practices but I promise you, we're doing it for all the right reasons."

"Then, I'm your girl," Cassidy said with a nod, moving to stand as she brushed off her jeans, pushing the hair up and out of her face. "But, I'm exhausted," she said with a yawn, stretching her small frame out as Sebastian also stood, gazing down at her. "Come and get me bright and early tomorrow and we'll do the whole debrief introduction thing," she added with a quick nod.

"Right, meet you at noon then," he teased, watching as she walked back over the invisible barrier through her door. She laughed and nodded at his comment, watching as the red pulsed angrily over his frame. Despite being from the same Origin, Sebastian's magic looked upset and angry. The red was a bit darker than most, possibly showing the weakness he had to wanting to use. Without another blink of her eyes, he was gone, the dust of red in the spot that he left fading away just as quickly as it was there.

Chapter 16

hey're not gonna kill you, you know," Sebastian teased as they walked up the cobblestones to the rather large mansion of a house in front of them. The exterior was old, probably built in the early 1900s and hadn't been taken great care of. The vines wrapped themselves aggressively around the stone, as if it were trying to strangle it as tightly as the plant could. The lawn was mowed, at least, and the paint was rather dark. If she were to walk by such a house daily, she would automatically steer clear of it. Whether it was meant to put off a terrifying charm or if it was just a coincidence, that was exactly the feeling that Cassidy was embracing at the moment.

"You didn't say that the League was holed up in the Addams Family mansion," she said teasingly, pushing the hair out of her face as they walked in tandem up the short bit of steps. Each step was recorded in Cassidy's mind. How many steps it took to walk from the street to the door, anything that was of possible importance with the outside integrity of the building itself. It was safe to assume that the League knew better than to just let her walk in off the street without any true form of security but so far, she didn't see much of anything.

Sebastian chuckled, grabbing the door handle and pushing it open, waiting for her to follow him but Cassidy stopped at the doorframe.

"You have to invite me," she reminded him, knowing that the barrier would keep her from crossing the threshold and before Sebastian was able to say anything else, he reached out and yanked her through the doorway, their bodies pressing against one another as the whimper erupted from Cassidy's throat. Her body tensed up, her eyes clamping shut until she was through the door, peeking out through her eyelid when she saw how close she was to him. One hand lifted and smacked him dead in the chest as she put space between the two of them, her cheeks bright blood red.

"You are an asshole!" she said, frustration rolling off of her in waves while Sebastian couldn't hold in the laughter.

"The house is in a human's name. We're not a great sanctuary if those who we want to save can't just come in to seek solace," he said with a shrug, rubbing his chest where she had hit him but thoroughly enjoying the fact that he was able to get under her skin. He couldn't decide if he was more thrilled by the possibility of taking her from his brother or just to be able to see if he could intrigue her at all.

"Well, how am I supposed to know that?" she said, her face speaking volumes about how angry she was with him. Her heart was still eagerly pounding against her ribs, the blood flow making her head slightly dizzy but she simply brushed it off. With what she was about to go through, she needed her efforts to be stronger than ever.

The home on the inside looked rather lack luster. Cobwebs littered the walls from lamps to couches, the smell of musty old dust so strong she could nearly taste it. If she were honest, the entire home looked like it hadn't been touched in decades.

"This doesn't inspire a bunch of confidence, ya know?" she said, reaching out a wiping her finger across the dust on the shelf, coughing slightly as Sebastian walked away from her, deeper into the house. "That doesn't mean just leave me!" she said quickly, her stride forcing her a few feet behind him but she was quick enough to keep up. The pair managed to get to a round room, one with each Origin symbol evenly spaced out within the circle. It was clear that the five origins were organized in a way to create a symbol of its own.

"Whoa," she said softly, her fingers instinctively tracing over the Epsilon symbol. The paint was faint but the faded hunter green was clear enough for her to see. Before she knew it, the green was pulsing over her fingers, the colors matching perfectly before she glanced over to Sebastian. Cassidy hadn't noticed that the man was scrambling with other things in the room and it took her a moment to notice what he was doing. Next to each symbol was a white pillar candle. Sebastian went from candle to candle, in a particular order, and lit each one before all five candles had a flame dancing back and forth. Sebastian motioned for Cassidy to walk back to the center of the room and the pair watched, each symbol glowing its respective color all on its own until all five were echoing against the walls. Cassidy blinked a few times, staring from the walls to Sebastian and by the time her eyes opened one more from her blink, the entire room had shifted. Where symbols on the wall used to be, doors leading to channeling rooms now existed. The room that they were now standing in was the rotunda that the other League members were talking when Cassidy was here the last time.

The new room was far warmer than the other one she was in. The lights were at least on, books strewn across the table closest to her and Cassidy immediately snapped her head to find the Epsilon channeling room, to her left. She could feel the pull towards the room but she needed to fight it for the moment. There was time to go in there later.

"A little paranoid, are y'all?" Cassidy teased but Sebastian's face refused to move. Before he was able to even retort, Geneva, Caleb and someone she had yet to meet walked down the hall towards them. It was clear by Geneva's face that she was the least excited person to see Cassidy standing next to Sebastian. If she were being honest, she was hoping that the whole wanting to become a League member was something she'd flake out on come morning.

"I like to think the right amount of paranoid," Geneva said as Caleb and Joseph, the man that Cassidy hadn't met yet, sat at the chairs in front of their respective origins. Joseph sat closest to Sebastian, next to the Chi Origin, and thus Cassidy assumed that he belonged there. Caleb managed to show her a genuine smile at her presence in their compound. If anyone could've brought her there, it was his words.

"Right," Cassidy said, clearing her throat and looking from Geneva to Sebastian. "I trust he managed to inform you as to what's going on?" She arched a brow as she watched how Geneva reacted. The heavy sighed left Geneva's lips, plopping a seat behind the desk.

"He told me that you haven't picked a side at all and want to go on a soul searching adventure with us," she said, condescendingly.

Cassidy clenched her fists and tightened her jaw, managing a snide chuckle at Geneva's comment. Before she could speak, Geneva continued.

"No... you don't get to stand there and laugh when what I'm saying is the truth. This is far bigger than you, pretty pretty princess. You might be some precious gift to the Exodus. You might very well be the special snowflake that everyone thinks you are but this is a war. It might not have hit you like it has us yet, you may not know the world that you've stepped into but the shit that goes down in here, we take very seriously," she said, pushing herself up and walking to stand in front of Cassidy. The women were the same height, a stark contrast between the brunette and blonde hairstyles but both women, whether they knew it or not, were glowing a hint of green.

"Ohkay, break it up you too," Caleb said, moving in between the two women and pulling them apart from one another.

"You have no idea what I've been through. You don't know who I am and even if you knew me before, that's not me anymore. So, how about you throttle back your sass and try being nice for a change. It might help with the wrinkles," Cassidy snapped back, taking a step back when Caleb stepped in the way. Both Sebastian and Joseph were content with watching the women go at it, keeping their heads out of it entirely.

Geneva managed to crack a smile, albeit begrudgingly, at Cassidy's wrinkle comment, watching Cassidy for another moment before walking back to her seat and sitting back down. "You're not going to be allowed to be around here without someone with you at all times, not until you've broken your connection with your Origin inside the Exodus. Until you do that, you will have the rights and privileges of a guest in this place." Geneva fiddled with her nails, fixing one before moving to the next.

Cassidy accepted the temporary freedom, knowing damn well that she needed to prove herself worthy of anything more. Somewhere down the line, she'd have to show her dedication without severing her connection to the Exodus or to Chase. That glimmer would hopefully present itself sooner rather than later. "Got it. No place by my lonesome," she said, moving to the Epsilon channeling room and leaning against the threshold.

"Those are off limits too," Geneva added and even Sebastian perked up at that one.

"You don't think that's a little extreme, Gen? I mean, regardless of what side she's with or could be with, the channeling rooms are sacred," Sebastian reasoned, watching as Joseph shifted closer to his own Chi channeling room. It took an incredible amount of energy to even create a proper one in the first place and to keep someone from their abilities wasn't something Sebastian could stomach watching.

"And, until we can trust her loyalties, she'll be held to a short leash. I'm not going to have someone who decides to go Exodus sit here and channel to become stronger, I'm sorry," she said with a shrug and Cassidy took a step forward, running her tongue over the bottom of her lip.

"I get it. Is there anything I can do while I'm here?" Cassidy asked passive aggressively, putting on the best fake smile she could manage. Geneva laughed, looking from the three men then looking to her.

"We'll find a way for you to be useful," she said, her smile growing, only to be cut off by the throbbing alarm sound filling the entire room. The alarm was deafening, causing Cassidy to cover her ears and grimace as the others seemed to be responding to the noise.

"What the hell is that?" Cassidy exclaimed, eagerly following after them down the halls. A handful of others moved to respond to the alarm, others that she had never seen before except for one. Jon. She quickly panicked that he heard her proposal about being a double agent but remembered that he was gone before she ever was able to get that out. The last thing he saw from her was her throwing up at what The Elder did to him.

"We have Chis trained to search for trigger pulses. When someone gets triggered, we get an alert. Then, we try to be the first person there to explain it all to them," Caleb said as some of the Chis red magic spread across the room in front of her. There were a handful of computer screens, the red sparking when the Chi, Joseph, brought the information to the forefront. There was a bright spike of green which she anticipated coming from Geneva but she was surprised when she saw another female, jet black hair and darker makeup, using her Origin. The green seeped into the computers, altering the electrical design of the hub and controlling it to do her bidding. It was one thing to watch one of the standard elements be manipulated by an Epsilon but it was apparent there were avenues that she hadn't truly delved into just yet. A whole plethorea of untapped potential.

"Why?" Cassidy asked, watching as they pinpointed information on the screens in front of her. What did it matter that they tracked freshly triggered people? To Cassidy's knowledge, they needed people who already picked their Origin and people that seemed to already know what they were doing magically.

"Because, stopping someone from ever believing the bullshit that the Exodus feeds them is easier than trying to sway them. It keeps them from needing to rip themselves away from their Origin, there's a lot of elements that we'd like to try to avoid," Geneva said, crossing her arms over her chest. Cassidy had to hand it to her, it honestly sounded as if she cared about someone other than herself.

"I know, it's hard to imagine her having a heart," Sebastian teased and the green lightning spark left Geneva's hand and absorbed itself into Sebastian's shoulder, getting a yelp of pain from the man for a brief second before clearing his voice and rubbing the spot that was now throbbing. Cassidy couldn't help the snicker that left her lips, moving closer to the screen and watching as the person became clearer as the information rolled in. The person on the screen had their entire social media and medical history pulled. It appeared that she was nineteen, brown eyes, dark hair with a rather interesting police history which seemed to lead to her death. Most of her police rap looked to be domestic violence, although the photos that were associated showed injuries on both sides. And, her cause of triggering appeared to be asphyxiation due to being strangled. The medical team was there quick enough to resuscitate her and trigger her abilities.

"We've got about ten minutes until Exodus gets to her. Sebastian, take the newbie with you, see if she can be persuasive enough out in the field to reel her in," Geneva said, pointing to Cass which caused her to shrug. Sebastian looked like he wanted to question being the one going out to grab someone new, especially when he was being so pushed magically, lately, but obliged without much backtalk and led Cassidy down the hall towards the rotunda room once again.

"You know, someone else can take me? Caleb or Joseph or someone else, you don't have to go," she said gently, trying to build some semblance of a relationship with the man. He seemed to be broken enough to be the in she needed to get closer to the League. Working an inside angle would only go so far unless she had someone who believed in her.

"It can't be someone else but, thanks for the suggestion," he said with a small grin, reaching his arm out to her and tugging her close which caused the blood to pool in Cassidy's cheeks. She pushed back to widen the gap and Sebastian just laughed, licking his lips. "I need you to be close to teleport. It's sort of the point," he said in a teasing tone and Cassidy narrowed her eyes, shaking her head.

"So maybe next time lead with that instead of just getting grabby," she muttered, moving to close the space once more.

"Duly noted," Sebastian said, laughing as the red Chi magic spread across his skin and wrapped the two of them up, moving to the outskirts of the hospital within a blink of an eye. Cassidy's breath caught in her throat, forcing her to lean against Sebastian as the magic started to fade away. "You alright?" Sebastian asked, taking a step and looking her over before Cassidy opened her eyes and nodded.

"Yeah, yeah, I'm alright. Just a little dizzy, I guess," she said softly, glancing over his shoulder towards the hospital and taking another shaky breath. "Time to go convince someone who just died that her entire life has changed," she laughed, squeezing his arm and pulling him towards the hospital, Sebastian falling into step next to her.

"How about I do the talking part? You pitching the League when you haven't even really picked us might not be the most sound defense," he reasoned to which Cassidy sighed and nodded her head.

The couple walked through the halls, Cassidy making up some lie about being the newly triggered woman's sister in an effort to get them up to her room.

"Don't even need to be a Chi to get us in," she said teasingly, glancing over her shoulder at him when he grabbed her and pulled her against the hall before she rounded the corner. Her heart filled up her throat, biting down hard on her bottom lip to prevent her from squeaking out in surprise.

"The Exodus is already here," Sebastian said, glancing to Cassidy and then back towards the newly triggered woman's room and then back to Cassidy, narrowing his own eyes at her.

"You let them know, didn't you?" he threatened, still hiding behind the corner but standing up taller. "The Exodus Chis have always done a poor job on locating newbies, it was the one thing we always managed to do better than they ever could." Sebastian knew why they were so damn good at it but it was still something that was rather unknown to most. Sebastian sacrificed his own sanity toward the efforts of helping the League win in the war that was started between the two factions. He channeled in his magic to help 24/7 in searching for someone out there that was triggered. No one in the Exodus was willing to give up that amount of energy on a daily basis but Sebastian knew both the risks and the rewards of doing what he was doing. He knew how much of a help his sacrifice was.

"What?!" Cassidy said quickly, glancing over Sebastian's shoulder to see who was visiting the woman already. "I didn't—I've been with you the whole time! I literally haven't left your sight!" she pleaded and Sebastian pressed her up against the wall, forearm underneath her chin as he watched her intently, trying to get a read off of her.

"That doesn't mean you didn't tell Chase. You are continuously attached to him at all times. It'd be easy to send something over to him," he said and Cassidy narrowed her eyes, shoving him off of her. Her heart was pounding but only because he was threatening her, not that she was lying. Sebastian watched her, letting out a sigh as he glanced back towards the woman who was no longer laying in bed.

"Come on," he grumbled, grabbing her hand and Cassidy ripped it away, following after him to try and catch whoever came to greet her. Cassidy was surprised that he dismissed his accusation so quickly but she wasn't in a place to disagree with him at the moment.

Several steps down the hallway, walking at a brisk pace, Cassidy could hear his voice, knowing it better than anyone else's. Chase's. Her hand came up to Sebastian's arm and she squeezed it, getting him to look back at her.

"Don't hurt him," she asked softly, continuing after him before reaching the couple outside. Chase and the woman's backs were to them, Chase's hand at the small of her back and the red magic pulsing into her skin. Cassidy felt the wave of jealousy instantly rip through her and she thought it was strange to see the red pulsing from his hand but she was so overcome with anger at his hand placement that she couldn't see much else.

"Brother, we've gotta stop meeting like this," Sebastian said, ensuring his closeness to Cassidy not only as a precaution to getting them both out of there but also to piss Chase off. Chase turned, the two facing Cassidy and Sebastian and the recently triggered woman looked both terrified and was partially hiding behind Chase's shoulder for protection.

"We're not here to hurt you," Cassidy said softly, taking a few steps forward to the girl and Chase laughed.

"Cass, she chose her side. You might not have had such a decisive thought on the matter but she's ours. It'd be safe for you two just to leave and let us be. For everyone," he said, straightening up in front of them and Cassidy had to swallow back her dislike at his behavior. She knew how this game needed to be played. She knew that she needed to keep a section of her off on the sidelines, taking what Chase was saying with a grain of salt. He was playing a game that she just simply needed to play better.

Sebastian watched Cassidy and Chase as closely as he could, taking in their demeanor towards one another, watching Cassidy who was far more telling than she let on. It appeared that each comment Chase had for her honestly affected her.

"There's a difference between her picking that side and you making her pick it, Chase," Sebastian said, noting how trusting the young woman already seemed to be with his older brother. It was like he won her over in seconds. "Skipping the free will part already, are we?" The chuckle left his lips, and he glanced over to Cassidy and then back to Chase. Cassidy watched the brothers for a moment, looking from Chase to the woman and then back to Chase once again. It was clear that the accusation honestly made her angry. The possibility of everything being against their will made her stomach churn.

"Believe what you will, Bas, I'm saving her from living on the run with all of your lot. Not having a community, not having a family... who would want that? Who would want to feel so empty with what we can provide everyone? She made her choice, it's time for us to get her there," he said, fully standing in front of the woman, Cassidy narrowing her eyes at him as he spoke. There were times before that Chase found a way to make her upset but this was beyond all before. The fact that her own mind had been bent in ways that made all of her previous memories false already made her sick to her stomach at the possibility of taking away someone's free will but for Chase to be so flippant about taking away the newbie's choice made her want to vomit.

"We're not letting you take her, Chase," Cassidy said, taking a step forward as she stared him down. She pushed waves of her own anger out through their bond, Chase adjusting his feet when he started to feel it. It was a strange sensation for the pair but it was obvious that it fed into their abilities.

"Well, I'm not going to just let her go without at least trying so, if you two wanna go, by all means." Chase took a step forward, rolling his shoulders and Cassidy glanced over to Sebastian, the rolls of anticipation radiating off of her skin, bond or not. It was clear that Cassidy was overwhelmed with anger and terror all in one and Sebastian reached his hand over to her, gave it a squeeze before they took a few steps towards Chase. Chase wasn't blind to the move, hands igniting bright red and sending out a powerful red blast in Sebastian's direction but he countered, taking his Chi abilities and teleporting to the other side of Cassidy. He would be lying if he wasn't going to try and stay close to Cassidy if only to protect the two of them. There would be no way he would mortally injure someone he was still bound to.

Cassidy let go of the pent up waves of green, the emerald color glowing brighter and more vibrant than ever before as she faced Chase, bright streaks of lightning erupting from the sky above them and heading straight for Chase. The rather experienced man anticipated the weather attack from her, moving to avoid each strike except for the last which struck his left arm which cause a wail of pain. He swallowed through the pain, Cassidy also adversely affected by the attack before he sent a wave of red towards her chest, knocking her nearly fifty feet back. Sebastian's head snapped up at the sound of Cassidy's body hitting the ground away from him and the red flared up even brighter in his hands, teleporting to Chase and then men colliding against one another.

"She won't trust you forever. You'll lose her before you know it," Sebastian spat at Chase, getting a few good punches to the face, one undercutting his jaw before Chase suckered back and caught a good right hook to the side of his face.

"And you think you'll be able to have her trust? Good luck. She loves me," he whispered, punching him once more, crumpling Sebastian to the ground as he lifted his head to find where Cassidy was. What he didn't anticipate was her already being behind the freshly triggered woman, ready to leave with her in an instant.

"Cass, give her up," Chase said, taking a step towards the two women when Cassidy held a knife from her boot to her stomach, ready to drive the metal into herself as a means to hurt Chase, if need be. It was a desperate move, it was a dangerous one but it would do a few things for her cause. It would get the League to trust her, it would harm Chase enough to get back to the League without any more incident and she would be fine once an Omicron got to her. In their lives, such an injury was a piece of cake. "Cassidy, look at yourself," Chase said, his voice calming down as he tried to close the space. Never in a million years would he anticipate Cassidy harming herself willingly to get what she wanted. Sebastian scrambled to his feet to watch the events in front of him unfold, his eyes closely watching the knife in Cassidy's hand. Her hand was steadily shaking, the terror of majorly causing herself harm and the hope that Sebastian would be quick enough to grab them before Chase caught up with her.

"Chase, I promise you, I'll do it. Take a step back, now, and let us go," she said, dragging the woman with her free arm as she took steps backwards away from him, the metal pressed against the fabric of her shirt. Chase's hands seemed to start growing red and Cassidy's heart rate accelerated. "If you even dare to go into my head, I swear to God, you'll regret it for the rest of your life," she said, trying to cover the pain in her voice. Regardless of what he needed to do to help prove her cover, there was a part of her that was starting to believe that Chase would do whatever it took to do right by the Exodus. Chase looked up at her and shook his head, the red growing stronger.

"You won't remember it," he said softly before the red grew around him. Cassidy shoved the knife cleanly into her left side, swallowing back a groan and the adrenaline was pumping through her veins enough so that the pain didn't hit her instantly but it did Chase. And that was what she was counting on. The red that had surrounded him dimmed for a moment as he gripped his stomach, feeling the metal slip through Cassidy's flesh and the pain was almost unbearable. He wasn't hurt himself and he wasn't bleeding but the pain was agonizing enough to make him buckle giving Sebastian long enough to teleport to the two women and before Chase was ready to look back up, the three were long gone.

"Damnit!" Chase groaned, the red teleporting him back to the Exodus empty handed.

Sebastian arrived with Cassidy and the woman, passing off the newbie to one of the front centuries that was patrolling the outside grounds. It was rare that the building had anyone on the outside since the inside was difficult to get into but with them out and knowing that they'd come up against the Exodus sooner or later, they implemented a wider perimeter.

"You're insane, you know," Sebastian muttered to her as he leaned her against the table, Cassidy pulling the knife out of her stomach and letting it clatter to the ground as Sebastian arranged the candles in the origins in the right pattern to move into the next layer of the League. She groaned when she glanced down at her hand, the blood soaking not only her shirt but her hand rather quickly, dripping down her pants and to her boots rather quickly. "You pulled it out? I thought you're not supposed to do that!" Sebastian said exasperatedly, picking Cassidy up in his arms and walking the few feet with her to the room where he could hear all the voices coming from.

"Some help here!" he called out, Caleb and Joseph clearing off the table that was in front of them as Sebastian hoisted her body up on the tabletop. Sebastian's shirt now had Cassidy's blood all over it, it was smeared on his hands as he put pressure on the wound, awaiting the response of one of the Omicrons within the League. It wasn't common that many came back with mortal wounds when up against the Exodus. Many were mental afflictions, ones that were impossible to cure or even help. And, many, didn't come back at all.

Flora stormed down the hallway, her jet black hair pulled up into a high ponytail making her cheek bones even more prominent. Cassidy remembered the woman vaguely from her very first trip into the League, when she was kidnapped. The two hadn't spoke since she came back to the League but now was as good a time as ever.

"What the hell happened?" Flora asked, pushing the sleeves of her black t-shirt up to her elbows as the bright blue magic pulsed over her hands, the color intensifying her own blue eyes. Her hands quickly moved over Cassidy's wound, trying desperately to heal her.

"The Exodus managed to get there before we did. Chase was there. And Cassidy had the brilliant idea to stop Chase from getting the drop on the both of us by stabbing herself and using their bond as a means of distraction." Sebastian sighed, watching Flora work on Cassidy, taking a step back and starting to pace. "It worked, at least," he mumbled with a quiet laugh, staring at the blood on his hands. It was odd to see his hands so red and it not be magic induced.

"Well, that's a way to get shit done, why hadn't we thought of it earlier?" Geneva laughed, watching as Cassidy came to on the table, the blood having soaked through her shirt and on to the table top. "Too bad she was probably the reason why the Exodus knew beforehand," she said, staring down the woman which got a rise out of Sebastian.

"She just saved the person we were after and injured herself in the process, give her some damn credit! Besides, I had the same concern. She had no idea, I know, I checked. She wasn't lying," Sebastian said as Cassidy took in a deep breath, rising quickly on the table and Flora put a soothing hand on her shoulder, quietly edging her to lay back down.

"It's okay. You're fine but you lost a lot of blood, alright? I'm fantastic at what I do but there are some things that I can't do instantaneously and you're going to feel a little woozy for a bit," she said, her voice calm enough to send waves of comfort over her, her heart rate settling just enough at her words. Cassidy blinked a few quick times, glancing from Flora to Sebastian and then to Geneva before speaking.

"I didn't tell them anything, I promise. I was kind of interested in seeing how we were going to pitch the League to a woman who had no idea what was going on. I didn't double cross you," she said, swallowing hard as her hand went to the knife wound on her stomach, a gentle red scar having already formed but the space was still tender to the touch. It wasn't perfect but it was far better than dying.

"You might not have told them that that was what you were doing but you have to believe that they simply lowjacked you. Why do you think it was Chase that they sent out? Because he's hot and easily convincing? No, it's because they knew you were coming, they knew that he'd be able to get to you and if he couldn't, he'd be able to find a different way to convince you," Geneva said, running her hand in the air to Cassidy. "And now you had to go and injure yourself when this could've been avoided all together if you'd just broke your bond, gave them up and sided with us."

"You're the one that sent me!" Cassidy yelled, sitting up with a whimper but pushing through it when others came to caution her. "You told me to go with Sebastian, you sent me to go help recruit so if you were this wise, you should've known better in the first place. I don't know when I shoved such a large branch up your ass but I think you can come off it anytime now and realize I'm not the damn enemy!" Cassidy growled, thoroughly over Geneva's shit with everything.

Geneva grabbed Cassidy's arm, pulling her so that she came closer to the edge of the table, locking eyes with the woman. "I do not trust you. We do not trust you. You are not one of us no matter how quickly you're willing to sacrifice yourself for the good of the others. So feel free to jump off of the 'I'm the best ever' train and swallow back your pride for a while, buttercup. We didn't create this group to play. We created it to win and winning is what we do. You have to earn everything else the way the rest of us did." She released Cassidy's arm and looked to Sebastian. "Make sure she stays rested as she heals, we'll talk later," she said before leaving the room, the anger leaving with her as the rest of the group settled down, offering Cassidy their congratulations for thinking so quickly on her feet.

"How about next time we take the less radical approach?" Sebastian teased once she seemed to have settled, watching her grimace as she moved around a bit. Flora did a wonderful job but she had to be mindful of how much of her Origin she used all at once. Bringing someone back from a wound got harder and harder and if the Exodus decided to attack, she didn't want to weaken herself too much.

"I guess I'm a more, go big or go home kinda gal," she laughed, reaching out and grabbing his arm to ease herself off of the table and to the ground. Her outfit was clearly ruined, as was Sebastian's but at the moment, she was more focused on how she felt like she'd been hit by a freight train.

"I guess I'll be pushing for the go home sort of time," he said, watching with a grimace as she slid off of the table. His hands were covered in her dried blood and his shirt had a nice size blood stain across the abdomen but he was just more concerned with the fact that she was alright over everything else.

"Hopefully we'll be better next time," she said as she moved to walk, each step a little less painful than the next but she was obviously uncomfortably sore.

"You know, we could say fuck the rules and let you go into the Epsilon room. It'll make it feel less... shitty," he said, nodding to the green walled room and Origin symbol down the hallway towards the rotunda. He'd probably take one heck a verbal lashing from Geneva but, in his eyes, she deserved as much help as she could get. Possible mole or not, she helped deliver a possible asset at that mattered to everyone.

"Geneva would have your head if she knew you even

suggested it," she laughed, leaning back against the table and shaking her head in denial. "I'll be okay. It'll just take me a while to not feel like I've been hit by a tank." She said, running her own bloody hand through her hair, thankful for the moment that her hand was at least dry.

"Nope, we went your way on the whole getting the asset part of the day, the least you can do is listen to me now and make you feel marginally better," he said, grabbing her arm to help her down the hall and she was too tired to truly argue with him. If Geneva found out, there were enough members inside the League that would argue in her favor.

Cassidy held on to the door, glancing from Sebastian and taking a step into the room and the groan fled from her lips before she could even attempt to stop it. When she expected Sebastian to leave her alone inside the room, she didn't anticipate him following after her, helping her walk through the room despite the negative effects he'd feel from sitting in an Epsilon channeling room.

"Sebastian, you don't have to stay in here, you'll feel like shit before you even realize it," Cassidy said, finding a nice sized couch and enjoying the cozy feeling that settled not only her nerves but every fiber of her being.

Sebastian knew it would be hard to tell the changes that the Epsilon room would make on him as time ticked by but it was worth it for him to stood where he stood, despite what he'd feel like afterwards. It wasn't something he wasn't already used to.

"You worry about you, let me worry about me, alright?" he said, sitting across from her, glad to see that it seemed to be working enough for her to calm down more.

"You're mad at him, at Chase," Sebastian said after a few moments of letting Cassidy absorb what the room could give her.

It really was a Godsend, what channeling rooms could do for that Origin. Sebastian could feel the oncoming feeling of his hands wanting to shake but he subdued it enough so that

Cassidy wouldn't notice.

"I don't know what I am with Chase," she said with a gentle laugh, shaking her head and resting her cheek against her knees with a heavy sigh. "I thought that I knew him, that I knew what he stood for, that he wouldn't..."

She swallowed, clearing her throat. "I had my entire history erased from me. I don't know what's real... I don't know what is fake. I don't even know my own damn Dad anymore and..." She took in a deep breath. "To have him seemingly willing to just alter my memory to get his own way, that's..." She licked her lips and looked up at him, trying to process through the night's events. "Terrifying," she finished, her thumbs running against the comfort of her jeans.

"That's why you came here, though, isn't it? Even if you didn't know what you were going to find, we offer a way to show you that they're not such a happy family. You have your doubts just like we all did." Sebastian tried to offer some semblance of good faith, knowing that she wouldn't feel better until she found a way to speak to Chase.

"Is there a way to block it?" Cassidy asked, strengthening the hold on her legs as she watched him. It was never a thought that she thought she needed to handle but obviously, it was something she was suddenly curious about. The privacy of her own thoughts and mind were hers, and hers alone. And she'd prefer to keep it that way.

"Not that I know of." He swallowed. "Wherever this all started, someone somewhere made sure that only one can control one Origin. A Chi can read another's mind and vice versa. We've learned how to cover it, to think of other things to confuse someone getting into our heads but there's no known way to do it. Yet, at least," he said, standing up and quickly shoving his hands into his jeans to prevent from showing how much they were shaking.

"You rest and let me know when you want to go back home and I'll get you there. You might feel like a prisoner but, I promise you, we just want to keep everyone safe." Sebastian watched her until she nodded, walking to the edge of the Epsilon doorframe, glancing back at her.

"Sebastian?" she said, watching him and cracking a smile. "Thanks, for staying with me," she said before he nodded his head towards her.

"Anytime."

Nearly twelve hours later, Cassidy woke back up with a start. The woman who electrically manipulated the screens when the newbie was found was inside the Epsilon channeling room had picked her up and was dragging her out of there as quickly as she could.

"Hey!" Cassidy yelled, clamouring to her her feet and instinctively bringing the green Origin to attack her but the woman let go of her and pushed her against the wall, trying to keep her voice low.

"Look, I let you sit in there as long as I could but Geneva is bound to go in there soon and having you caught in there is far worse than me dragging you out," she said, trying to calm Cassidy down. She nodded, straightening up and smoothing out her clothes that were now sticking to her body, the blood stains practically burned into the material.

"No, you're right, you just startled me," she said, glancing to her hands as the woman took a step back.

"Jane, by the way." She looked Cassidy over and shook her head. "Come on, let's get you cleaned up and fresh clothes on. It'll help," she said and Cassidy cracked a smile, following after her. "Don't take Geneva so seriously. She doesn't do well with competition, whether it is another person in her Origin or someone that might take Sebastian's eye away," Jane laughed, the long strands of her black hair in a side braid that hit around her ribcage. Black jeans with a black shirt, black eyeliner and bright hazel eyes, Jane was probably a few years older than Cassidy but they had similar builds.

"What's that supposed to mean?" Cassidy laughed as the two walked, trying to remember the ways in which Jane led her down the maze of halls to her room.

"I mean, Geneva and Sebastian used to be a thing, long time ago. He spiraled pretty quickly after your Mom died and she seemed to do a pretty good job at distracting him for a while until he realized how much of a bitch she was. They haven't been together in over six months but there's still some hostility there and she's far too possessive. She doesn't enjoy sharing." Jane opened the door to find a rather lackluster room.

"There's nothing going on there. He helped save my ass and happens to be Chase's brother. Since I'm joined to Chase still, there's obviously some brotherly stuff going on that I don't really know all too much about." She shrugged, glancing around until she spotted the shower, pointing towards it.

"More than you could ever imagine, actually," Jane teased as she nodded, moving to grab up a towel and a wash rag. "I'll grab you some spare clothes, feel free to take your time. I'll be down in the cove if you need me," she said, gesturing over towards where the rotunda of channeling rooms were, leaving Cassidy alone once she left.

Cassidy glanced at the pair of jeans and black t-shirt that was on the bed before bringing herself to look at the mirror in the bathroom.

"Fuck," she muttered, bits of her makeup smeared on her face, her hair a mess piled on top of her head. The biggest point of staring at herself was to see just how her body had held up to her own attack against it. A lightning strike brand ran from the epicenter of her elbow to about halfway through her forearm. It was strange to see such a brand on her own body since she was able to control the element without harm but it was because the attack affected Chase that it had caused a scar to form. Her blue eyes locked on to the gaze in the mirror, leaning forward as she stared at herself. So much had changed over the past few months that she wasn't even sure the woman looking back at her was a woman she liked anymore.

Her fingers pulled at the fabric, slowly rolling it up towards the top of her head and dropping it to the floor in a rather unwanted pile on the ground. It took a bit more effort to shimmy out of her shoes and jeans but she was glad when the clothing was off of her. It made everything from the night before seem less real now that she wasn't in clothes that proved her memory to be right.

Using her abilities, it only took the water about half a second to reach the desired temperature she wanted, the water running a bright red color to a dull orange once her blood was rinsed off of her skin. The pool of water at her feet was a shade of orange, Cassidy sticking her head under the shower to happily rid her frame from the horrors of the night before. The few moments that she had beside herself caused her chest to heave, the worry, the terror, the anger, every emotion she had managed to bury deep within the pit of her stomach managed to break the surface and her hands were trembling as they pushed through her drenched hair. Each breath was harder and harder to take as she replayed the night in her head. Remembering Chase disregarding the woman's free will, his threat to take away her own if she didn't choose what he wanted her to. The cold metal piercing her skin—even if she didn't feel it in the moment, her memory of it was more vivid than she ever anticipated it could be. Having held in everything she'd experienced recently, it felt refreshing to just let out it.

A whimpered cry left her throat, leaning against the wall to hold her legs up as they begged to buckle, wishing that they could simply clamour to the ground and be free from the responsibility that she seemed to have. Her breaths started to become more and more labored, a lightheadedness creeping up through her mind and it was quickly taking longer to take in a deeper breath. The warmth of hives started to spread against her chest, taking the place of her normally pale skin. She could tell that she was having a panic attack but there didn't seem to be a way to calm herself down.

It was then that she felt Chase in her head, first in calming waves and then his voice. Her stomach flipped and churned at her body's automatic response to his invasion into her mind but she just couldn't push him out in the moment.

Cassidy, are you alright? Regardless of the fact that his words were only to be heard in her head, she could tell that there was a lingering worry brimming the surface under his words. It seemed genuine and it caused Cassidy's knees to finally give way, collapsing to the ground where she pulled her legs to her chest, letting the hot water to continue to cascade around her.

Get out of my head, Cassidy replied, her fingers running up through her hair as she cried, pulling at the ends as she still tried desperately to capture a breath. Chase's feelings that overwhelmed their bond did a mediocre job of settling her heart rate but the presence of them in the first place caused her anxiety to increase tenfold. The whole reason she was so unsteady at the moment was what he was putting her through.

Cass, don't shut me out. You wanted to go work the other side. I have to hold up appearances. Cassidy, tell me you're alright. Chase's words didn't calm her down like she hoped that they would. Days ago, she wasn't worried about facing the challenges that being a double agent was going to cause her. She thought she understood the dangers, the things she was going to have to give up to make things safer for everyone but apparently that simple realization was harder to swallow than she ever imagined.

I just didn't think that seeing- that being on the other side of this would be so hard to watch. Seeing you, wondering if you were just that good of a liar... I need time, Chase. Even if she wasn't working on the other side, watching Chase lie without a blink of an eye, it was intimidating. There wasn't many times that she was able to be clear of Chase's influence over her. Even when she was by herself, he had the ability to come in and soothe her, rile her up; it was an intoxicating relationship. Volatile. Deadly. It was becoming increasingly apparent how much she didn't truly know the man that she was attached to. Whether she was learning that from the distance posed between the two of them or simply time, the clarity was welcomed. Hell, she knew if she were having this conversation right in front of him, he'd manage to have her calmed and a puddle in his hands practically instantly. It wasn't that she was gullible by any means, she just trusted far too easily. Love and emotion impacted her in ways that were indescribable. The Exodus themselves fit her so well because there was a hole that she desperately tried to fill. With anything.

Just, leave me alone. She finished her sentence, disconnecting herself from their connection the best she could. There was no known way, at least to her knowledge, to shut it off completely but she knew that if she ignored him long enough, it would get easier. As long as she controlled her emotions, as long as she kept herself mellowed enough to survive, she would do just that.

Cassidy gazed at her hands, expecting to watch them shaking but they weren't. Perfectly calm, the water having ran clear by this point and she was able to take in a stable few breaths to settle the rest of her heart rate down. The realization was key to not only who Cassidy was but who she also wanted to be. No one could help her. No one could make her stronger or more powerful. She would need to be her own white knight at the end of the day. Standing up for what she believed in and putting her best foot forward was the only way she was going to keep sane through the world she was now living in. And, that was good enough for her.

She sat for another few minutes, her eyes closed as her body took the hot water as it impacted against her back, embracing both the good and bad pain it caused her. By the time she shut the water off, her skin had shriveled up into prunes. As she toweled off, a quick glance to herself in the mirror was rather refreshing.

"I'm stronger than this shit," she said, watching as her face finally agreed with the statement because, at the end of the day, she was. "No matter what happens, remember that," she said, pointing to herself and cracking a small smile, finishing drying off the rest of her body. Cassidy pulled on the clothes that Jane had found for her, thankful that the women were similar shapes and returned to the rest of the group down the hallway in the cove.

Chapter 18

How's she doing?" Joseph asked, the main members of the League seated around a round table in the center of the Cove. It'd been roughly a month since Cassidy decided to move in full time with the League. Her connection to the Exodus was still in tact as was her bond with Chase but it was only a matter of time until she was convinced otherwise to break those lasting ties. She was noncompliant to her double agent duties for the first week in the League but it didn't take long to convince her that the info was necessary. Much like the Chancellor had tried to explain to her, this was bigger than one side versus the other. This encompassed all five origins abilities to stay stable. Neither group could continue on in a means to blow each other off of the map entirely. She agreed to give detailed information to the Exodus in exchange that no one in the League would be harmed. Cassidy sought a way to convince both sides that they could exist in harmony. No war, no armies, simply life.

The Chancellor and the Elders had agreed to her terms and because so, Cassidy agreed to continue spying on them to hopefully find a way to convince them that fighting one another was simply too volatile for the whole. And while the Exodus seemed to be accepting Cassidy's newfound plan of peace and harmony between everyone, the League was still out for blood.

"Strung out, among other things," Caleb said, glancing into the Epsilon channeling room to find Yvette, the newbie that Cassidy and Sebastian managed to save from the Exodus, curled up on the floor, shaking violently. Once the history was explained to her after the pair saved her, she became the epitome of terrifying. Her Origin, Sigma, picked her almost instantly and it appealed to her soul more than any other. She was a troubled woman, full of hatred, full of a need for revenge and that was only fueled tenfold when she had the ability to manipulate life forces. The obsession into dismantling the Exodus was heightened by Geneva and her increasingly sadistic behavior and Yvette found herself using in heavy doses, needing more and more to just keep going. They were at a point that Yvette nearly was caught using against humans out in town and that was when the League was forced to step in and handle the situation.

"Your Origin changes a person." Cassidy spoke up, a dark t-shirt clinging to her body with a pair of worn jeans and her hair up with a few messy curls surrounding her face. It was clear that she was battle worn, exhausted but there was an apparent strength to her that was far more noticeable than ever before. She was leaning back against the wall away from the table, her foot on the wall and arms crossed over her chest. It was clear that she wasn't allowed in the inner circle just yet, having her connections to the Exodus even still.

"Thank you, Captain Obvious," Geneva said but Cassidy pushed herself off, staring into the Epsilon room with an exhausted sigh.

"No, not origins, their Origin, Sigma. I might not wield it

but the few times I've felt it... it's dark and endless and that kind of power to someone already known to have issues is destructive," Cassidy said, staring at Yvette groan, unconscious but her body was still fighting her internal demons.

"It picked her for a reason though. I won't disagree with you but she can handle it. We just need to figure out a better way to help," Caleb said, rubbing the back of his neck. It was obvious that he had grown to care for her over the past few weeks, especially when there weren't that many Sigma in the first place to share stories with.

"I know that you want to have hope, Caleb, but we have to be smart here. She nearly killed a human and we can't have both the Exodus after us and the humans." Joseph piped up, leaning forward on his forearms and crossing his fingers out in front of him as he stared at the others. "I vote that we wipe it from her and help her that way," he said, leaning back in his chair and staring at the others. Some nodded but there were a few who had thoughts otherwise.

"Absolutely not! You can't-this woman's mind has already been played with! And, we still don't know if that has a negative effect in the future. It's her goddamn mind. If anything, we should be giving her reign over that," Cassidy argued and Caleb nodded in agreement. Geneva was obviously on Joseph's team, Jane seeming indifferent and Bryan seemed to agree with Cassidy. Sebastian was rather stoic, seated next to Joseph.

"And we can't have someone with her abilities be a nutcase either," Joseph argued which caused Cassidy to rub her face, frustrated with the entire outcome. Geneva started to speak but was quickly cut off by Cassidy.

"What if we try my way first. I go in, try and help her, give her a place to anchor to, guide her through it and if I can't—if I can't get her to hold on to the part of herself that she never dare to forget, you guys can have your way," she offered, watching their expressions. There literally wasn't much to risk, other than Cassidy herself but she wasn't seen as a great loss, at least not yet.

"Just because you've managed to handle getting Williams back on the train, doesn't mean you're some sensei able to fix everyone's problems," Geneva said, looking Cassidy over but Cassidy didn't give her another minute to argue back with her, already walking over to the Epsilon channeling room.

"Give me my time then I promise I'll give her to you," she said, disregarding anyone else who wanted to argue as she settled herself in the room, sitting in front of Yvette, placing her hand on her to wake her. The spark of green left her fingers, sending a short electric pulse into Yvette's skin and the woman came to rather quickly, scrambling to pull her knees to her chest.

"Cass? What's going on?" she asked, clearing her throat when staring at her hands which were trembling. She clenched her hands, begging her Origin to come to the surface, unable to conjure the magic at all and it was in that moment that she noticed that she was in another Origin channeling room. "Cassidy?" she asked, locking eyes with her.

"You nearly killed a couple out in town. You're here, in the Epsilon room to calm down for a little while, okay?" she said softly, reaching out and thumbing over the top of her hand. She shushed her softly, trying to get Yvette to focus on anything other than the need or want to use. "I know it's hard, I know," she said softly, squeezing her hands with a frown.

"I did what?" Yvette asked, the break in her voice nearly echoed in the room before she started to shake her head. "I didn't do anything, I don't remember anything," she said, clawing softly at her temples and Cassidy moved to grab her hands, pulling them into her lap and her green Origin spun over them, trying to settle the woman down.

"You don't remember?" Cassidy asked, reaching up and brushing back a strand of her hair as she watched her, shaking her head no rather vigorously.

"No. No, absolutely not. I know that I'm having issues but I would never," she swallowed hard, staring up at Cassidy with a face that had no idea what she had done. Cassidy watched as the terror set in, watching as Yvette came to terms with possibly losing herself to the abilities she'd grown to enjoy. A volatile nature was hard to break, especially when aided by such a strong and suggestive Origin like Sigma. Cassidy squeezed Yvette's hands, letting them go as the green Origin subsided around them.

"We'll get to the bottom of this, I promise, okay? Just, I'll be right back," she said, cracking a smile and leaving the room to return back to the cove. Yvette simply nodded, watching her body shake on the floor of the Epsilon channeling room.

Cassidy closed the door behind her, staring at the members sitting around the table, many of them surprised that she was back so quickly. Over the past month, Cassidy had picked up a knack of teaching better methods of control to others, using her Epsilon abilities to teach emotional Origin control. It seemed to be working for many but it took time, more time than Cassidy had just taken.

"Well, you've either gotten very good or she's worse than we thought," Joseph teased, clearing his throat when Cassidy seemed to be looking rather serious. Many of them leaned in, eager to hear what she had to say to them, all but Sebastian.

"You're here to tell us that you don't think she has anything to do with her losing control," Sebastian said, his eyes staring at his hands before lifting them to meet Cassidy's gaze. She took in a short breath and nodded her head, swallowing hard as she stared at Sebastian's demeanor. The man had changed far more than she ever thought possible over the past month. He'd been sleeping more, the gauntness in his cheeks seemed to be filling and there was a light in his green eyes that Cassidy never noticed until recently. Something within him was healing and Cassidy had herself to thank for much of that. Even without a bond.

Joseph glanced from Sebastian to Cassidy, arching a brow

between the looks he gave both of them before leaning back in his seat and laughing. It was a genuine laugh, a guttural desperate attempt to hear the words that were said and to hope to anything in the world that what he was putting together wasn't possibly true.

"You- you think they're getting to us... and we don't even know it?" Joseph finally said after he calmed himself, staring at the table and then down the room to Yvette, listening to her moans. Origin withdrawal was one of the biggest and deadliest killers to a triggered person there was. First there was the sickness that came with not using and then came the illness of using too much to compensate once you could use again. It was a drug in every shape of the word and it was their life blood. Some used it for good, some for personal gain and some simply because they wanted to make sure no one else could be better than themselves. If the Exodus were using Chis to come and manipulate existing members of the League to do terrible things, even worse than the things that got them kicked out in the first place, it would only be a matter of time until the League surrendered and the Exodus got their way. But, that wasn't possible. Chase and the others had promised Cassidy that they wanted harmony. They wanted a future where everyone could exist without issue, without hatred. Or, so she'd been told.

"I'm not sure yet, but, you look at her, you talk to her, she doesn't remember anything. It's like something just switched off in her head and I know how Origin addiction works, how it starts and how it starts to feel." She swallowed, her eyes finding Sebastian's quickly before looking back to the rest of the group. "I don't think that is what is going on here," she reasoned, running a hand over the back of her neck as she thought through what her options were. She knew that she needed to talk to the Exodus and confront them,. There were too many things that had come up over the past few weeks that she simply dismissed as coincidence or that it simply didn't make any sense but this... this was far too connected for her to just pass off as nothing.

"I'm going to go back to where she attacked those humans, see if I can get anything and then I'll be back," she said, all of them nodding except for Sebastian and Geneva. Sebastian seemed disinterested in the entire conversation, glancing off into the distance rather than paying any attention but it was clear that Geneva was just thoroughly done with everyone banding behind the possible prophet.

"You have two hours. Two hours and if you're not back, we're scrambling her memory like a good batch of eggs," Geneva said, her eyes unwavering as she stared up at Cassidy. The womEn held each other's gaze for a few moments before Cassidy turned on her heel and walked down to the hall towards the exit she was safe to use without an escort. It was only when she was down by the door to the outside that anyone even tried to stop her.

"You're going to see him," Sebastian said, grabbing her arm and pulling her back slightly. Cassidy sighed, removing her arm from his grasp before shaking her head. "You know he'll just lie and at the worst case, he'll make you forget that you ever even went the—"

"Chase wouldn't hurt me, not intentionally." She cut him off, crossing her arms firmly over her chest. "Now, I'm going to find out what's going on with Yvette. You should focus more on keeping her safe rather than what I'm doing," she said, her hand on the door to push it open. Sebastian reached out and grasped the handle, preventing her from opening the door.

"I'm worried about the one person too blind to worry about herself" he said, watching her reaction and growing more frustrated by the fact she wasn't seeing that she was being played. "Don't even try to lie to me right now. I know where you're going when you leave here. You're meeting with him. And, I know you might think that he's the one and that you were meant to be but believe me when I say, that's not where you're supposed to be," he said, staring her down and releasing the door. "You know it, you just won't let yourself admit it that you belong here, with us." He paused for a moment before continuing. "With me." Sebastian watched as the blood pooled in her cheeks, quickly shaking her head at his comment and taking a step forward into the door.

"If you thought I was interested, I'm sorry for leading you on. I was simply trying to help you. And right now, I'm trying to help everyone because I belong in a world where we all exist, equally and happily," Cassidy said, pushing through the door front. "And, don't follow me," she added, frustrated that he was able to get under her skin so easily.

Chapter 19

Chase took a full fifteen minutes to get to Cassidy's old home, which worried her even more than she ever thought possible. Dating someone who was able to teleport upon command, it rarely caused him to be late, let alone take longer than a minute to meet up with her. Every fiber of her being was worried that the entire conversation, she was going to be battling on the offensive, attacking Chase the moment he got there. Cassidy was begging with inch of her soul that it was just a misunderstanding, that Yvette was far more gone than anyone else had ever determined.

Instead of knocking on the door, Cassidy felt the warmth of his Origin before he even managed to appear in her kitchen, watching as the red slowly started to appear which was filled with his presence only seconds later. Without a word or even a breath, Chase moved across the span on the kitchen and pulled Cassidy into his arms, melting his lips against her own and her body responded instantly. Regardless of the reason for calling him, her soul and his were connected in the most primal of ways and while they managed to develop their affections for one another, almost every greeting began the way this one did. Cassidy nearly lost her own train of thought as Chase's fingers tangled up in her hair, his tongue dancing against her own and the spark of their origins ran over their skin like wildfire. Hearts beating as one, pounding faster against their ribcages as the kiss lingered, it wasn't until Chase separated for a moment for a breath that even a conscious thought passed over her own mind.

"Chase," she practically moaned, the name dripping from her lips as she tried to clear the fog that had settled in her mind. She ran her tongue over the bottom of her lip, blinking her eyes rather quickly and pulling out of his arms far enough so that she could regain some of her sanity.

"I just missed you," he whispered, rubbing the small of her back when she pulled away, swallowing hard. "We've been monitoring what's going on with some of your people out in public and I was worried that they'd found you out or something," he said, brushing the hair out of her face and managing a gentle smile in her direction. "Every time we leave here, I worry more and more that we won't make it back here," he admitted softly, Cassidy's face leaning into the cup of his hand and she turned her lips to kiss the inside of his palm. Sebastian was right, she shouldn't have came to see him. She should've gone straight to her father rather than try to get something across to Chase. She was biased.

"I'm fine," she said , pulling her head out of his hand and clearing her throat, moving to lean back against the kitchen counter before continuing. "We finally got ahold of Yvette, thank you for helping me find her. For some reason, no one could get a good read on her," she said, a hint of confusion at how that sentence sounded. How was it that people so close to her were unable to find her until she started to attack humans? "And then what she did to those people... we're all kind of reeling from it. She's secure, at least." Cassidy looked slightly broken as she spoke. It was clear that the few months she'd experienced in this world were enough to break her. It didn't matter what she found in the process, it was intense enough to change the person she thought she was, forever.

"I'm glad you managed to get her back and avoid such a big incident. Were your Omicron able to heal the humans or do you need me to send out some of ours?" Chase asked, arching a brow and Cassidy shook her head.

"No, we managed to fix the problems she made, we're just trying to help her now. The problem is, she doesn't even remember anything about that night." She frowned, looking up at Chase with a heavy sigh.

"That's not uncommon though, for someone as lost as she is. Losing time, losing memory, it's pretty par for the course, isn't it?" Chase said, trying to understand where she was going with all of this in the middle of a possible war. Wouldn't it be easier if she just brought Yvette to him and he could treat her?

"No, losing track of where you are isn't unheard of but, usually when someone is addicted as deeply as she is, they tell you what you want to hear in an effort to get out of a channeling room and have the chance to go out and use again," Cassidy said, staring more intently at the man in front of her than she ever did before.

"How can I help here, Cass? Did you just want to see me to calm yourself down or—were there other motives?" Chase asked, pushing himself off of the kitchen counter, taking a step closer to her. The action was surprising to Cassidy but not uncommon. The two managed to have a rather back and forth sort of relationship.

"It's just, we couldn't find her and you all could. And then there was the fact that she can't remember what happened or why she attacked people in the middle of the open public. I just didn't know if you knew more than you were letting on," she said, the sound of her heart beating filling in her ears and Chase closed the distance between the two of them, thumbing over her cheek before staring into her eyes.

"If you're asking if I had anything to do with it, look in my eyes when I say, I didn't," he said, his voice unwavering and his heartrate calm. Cassidy read his face, studying every inflection of his appearance before she deduced that he was being truthful. If the bond gave them one thing, it was the inability to truly lie to one another.

She breathed out an air of relief when she watched his reaction, thankful to whoever would listen that he wasn't some monster. It didn't clear the entire Exodus but knowing that he was there to defend and support her was more than enough strength that she needed.

"Oh thank God," she mumbled, leaning up to him and kissing him passionately, running her fingers through his hair and tugging him against her as she sighed against his lips. "I just don't know where I fit anymore. These people, Chase, they're not bad people," she said, her voice soft but shaking as she leaned in his arms. "They all have abilities and personalities that are fantastic and wonderful and they're not our enemy," she pleaded, knowing that he wasn't the one that she needed to argue with. It was her father and the rest of the Elders that needed to know that the League wasn't something to worry about. It was something to embrace. "We can't keep doing this, dividing us because of our pasts. I know these people did something that the Exodus deems irreprehensible but... Chase, these people are people. They deserve to be a family with the rest of us. They don't deserve to be treated as lepers. I can help them. I've learned how to help center those that lose control and I can bring them back, I promise you, I can." Cassidy stared up at Chase and was practically begging him to understand what she was trying to say. She might not have all the origins but it was seeming that she was the true prophet that was called for to bring great wonders to all.

Chase stared at her, listening to her heartbeat, watching her plead with him to listen to what she had to say. He didn't anticipate this being the outcome of having her undercover for over a month but it wasn't that far fetched.

"You know you don't have to convince me, Cass. Why don't you go back, tell them that the Exodus has proposed a immunity to those who were exiled on various terms. We can have the Elders and the League sit and chat and have the proposal actually on the table to end this silly battle before it ever really begins," he agreed, squeezing her hips where his hands were, lifting her up to his lips and kissing her once again.

"I love you," she said, lips still pressed against his when the words came pouring out of her mouth, far too slow to stop herself from spilling what was on her mind at the moment. Chase stared at her, his own smile growing along with the rate of his heart and he managed to kiss her again before even speaking.

"I love you," he said in return. "And you doing this can bring you back home. To me, to us, to everything the world has to offer us," he said softly, kissing her one last time. Never in a million years would Cassidy believe that she would be in such a position that she was in now. Madly in love, at the cusp of bringing about the best union ever known to the world and saving everyone she cared for in the process.

"It won't take me long. Most of them will be easy to convince. There are a few that will have something to say but, I'll win them over. And, maybe by tonight, we'll be able to sleep in the same bed once again," Cassidy said, her optimism spewing from every part of her body. Chase laughed, nodding his head and dragging her up to him and pressing his lips against hers, pressing through every ounce of compassion and emotion that he could muster up in that moment. Everything they'd ever known or experienced was culminating in this night and Chase never thought he'd see the day that it could all possibly come to an end. Despite knowing a history before the two factions, it seemed that living in a world looking over one's shoulder the entire time was the only way he thought he'd live for the rest of his life but his girlfriend showed another alternative. She showed a way out for everyone.

"Let me know when it's time," he whispered, setting her down and before she could respond, he was already disappearing into a red burst of energy. Cassidy's legs quickly took her to the door, ready to run back to the League and convince them that this was all going to be okay. The mirror by the door caught her eye, looking herself over one last time before embarking on what she thought was her goal in life.

"Time to make you proud of me, Mom. I won't fail you, I promise," she said, her appearance more and more like her mother every day she grew older and tonight was the night that everything in her life mattered more than ever. Tonight was the night that ended the pain that everyone who was exiled would ever feel.

The anticipation was intense and she didn't think that her heart could take any more waiting as she ran through the streets, trying to get back to the visitor entrance to the League. Unlike a true member, she had no ability to access it by herself which took that much longer to get back to their base headquarters. Even running all the way there, she managed to shave three minutes off of her best time, allowing her body to will itself to the finish line. She wasn't entirely sure what she was going to tell them to convince them to plead their cases to the Elders but she knew whatever she did say, she would win their hearts over. She had to.

Her fingers reached out towards the door handle, twisting the knob as quickly as she could and pushing herself forward through the door frame. She waited in the hallway, using her Origin to seep into the walls which switched her to the actual League headquarters. Someone would have to escort her in further if she planned on getting down to the Cove but since they were expecting her, she anticipated someone waiting at the entrance to help her through.

Except, no one was there.

Not only was no one there, the hallway was rather silent.

A pang of worry rolled through her, glancing around trying to figure out what in the world was going on. Cassidy bit on the inside of her lip, wondering if she should try Sebastian's entrance code further into the headquarters. She wasn't supposed to know how to get in by herself but she was simply an observant and resourceful woman who didn't like the fact that she couldn't go and come how she pleased. Her hands moved quickly, setting things into place to verify that it was Sebastian who was entering deeper into their home base and it was in that moment that she wished she would've never came back to the League HQ. When she expected to see people greeting her, she smelled burning flesh. Cries and screams echoed down the halls, a haze of various origins in the air as if recently used. She didn't know what had happened but one thing was clear.

The League as she knew it, was no more.

Cassidy ran to the first body on the ground that she saw. It was Jane, her long strands of black hair matted to the blood that was gushing from the side of her neck. From what she could tell, the blood was coming from some sort of animal bite.

Her fingers clamoured along her body, trying to put pressure against the wound to keep her from bleeding out. Jane took in a sharp breath when Cassidy's fingers pressed against her wound, Cassidy letting out a shaky, hollowed gaspe.

"What happened?" she asked, the tremble in her voice clear as day. Cassidy kept her voice low enough so that she couldn't be heard in case whoever or whatever attack happened to still be nearby. Jane swallowed which caused another gush of liquid to come out of her throat, her hand moving to clasp over Cassidy's as she tried to speak.

"-dus, breached the cove, I—" she gasped, squeezing

Cassidy's hand as tight as she could, the green siphoning from Cassidy and into Jane as a hope that it would do anything to keep her alive. "You -ust stop -em" she said, her voice cracking at each word and it was hard for Cassidy to understand her at all.

"Jane? Jane, no no, please, I'll get Flora or someone, please, just hold on for me, please," she begged, leaning her head down to rest her forehead against Jane's, letting out a broken cry, tears cascading down her cheeks and hitting Jane's.

She could easily feel when Jane's life left her body, the pulse of their Origin subsiding and Cassidy simply felt alone again. A pit rose up in her stomach as she pulled her hands back, every inch of her palms covered in her blood. It took her a moment to push herself to her feet, willing herself to push back whatever she was feeling and to take on what was threatening those she'd grown to care about.

From what she could understand from Jane, it seemed as if the Exodus was to blame for such an attack which sent shock waves through her system. If it was, if it wasn't just some side group or someone wanting revenge then that meant that Chase was distracting her from the truth. He was playing her.

Cassidy looked down at Jane's body, swallowing back the sobs that begged to come to the surface as she willed herself down the hallway, one foot after the other. The green energy surged over her hands, Cassidy watching as the red blood mixed with the green color that sparked through her and there was a fire inside her that could no longer be quelled. She wasn't sure what the answers actually were anymore but she knew that the Exodus was not what they seemed to be. And, she'd deal with that after she dealt with whoever was trying to kill them.

Cassidy spied a Delta, an Exodus Delta, coming down the hallway from the Cove, a tiger on his heels with a silver glow around it. The man stopped instantly at the sight of her, taking in a sharp breath.

"You weren't supposed to be here," he said, slinking back to attack when Cassidy rose her hand in the air, the green intensifying and conjuring a large tree branch in thin air, instantly calling the branch to grow and she watched as it plunged into the chest of the man, his scream filling her ears. No emotion crossed her face as she killed the Delta. It was as if her body was operating on autopilot.

"She was my friend," she said , her voice monotone as her eyes finally landed on the man who was crumpled to the ground, deceased. If others thought that she was changed before with what she'd been through, things were about to change in ways that not even Cassidy understood.

By the time her legs took her to the end of the hallway and into the Cove, she saw that the rooms had been ransacked. Books and files were ripped apart, blood was smeared across the walls and the sigils for each Origin were scorched in the walls—which Cassidy assumed must've been connected in how they managed to breach their security. Besides Jane and the Delta, it was clear that no one else was in the Cove which only left her a few possibilities. There were survivors. They were in hiding. Or, they were captured.

"Caleb? Sebastian? Gen?" Cassidy called out, running down the hallway at this point, eager to find some semblance of life still within the walls of the League. Even hearing Gen's voice would be better than nothing.

She made it down the hall, away from the Cove and towards the room that she was living in for the past month. The first room she passed was Jane's, a sinking pull of regret swallowing her up but she pushed forward. Caleb's room as well as Joseph's and Flora's were all emptied, seemingly untouched.

It wasn't until she got to Sebastian's that she noticed any sort of distress at all. There was blood on the floor and the room was an entire disarray. The night table was overturned, the door nearly blown off its hinges.

It was apparent that he or whoever was in his room, put up one hell of a fight.

"No," she said, touching the door for a moment before her legs carried her to her room. Inside her room, her trunk and other various items were torn apart. Pictures were ripped in half, her bed was upside down. It was as if they were looking for something but couldn't seem to find it. Despite what her head was trying to wrap around, she knew there was only one thing to do at this point; Return home to the Exodus and make someone pay for what they'd done.

Chapter 21

oments like these, Cassidy hated that she couldn't just teleport to where she wanted to go. She was, however, thankful that she was at least able to use one of the League cars, driving as fast as she could to the entrance of the Exodus. It was such a different feeling, returning now like she was. The first time she came to the Exodus, she was coming for answers and guidance and for a family. And now, she was coming for answers, for revenge and for her family. It was such a twisted world that she found herself in, even after only a month's time. The Exodus had their rules for a reason and she understood that but there was no way the people she worked with and got to know over the past month did the deplorable things they were accused of and now that she nearly had proof that someone was framing them—like she had with Yvette—and the fact that someone within the organization managed to attack those she'd grown to love, that was enough of answers for her to act. This was far beyond just her anymore. The leaders, her father and the other elders, were allowing someone to disgust the name they worked so hard for and while she prayed that her father was oblivious to the entire thing, as Chase hopefully was, she was starting to have to accept the evidence presented in front of her. If only she'd listened to Sebastian when he told her not to go in the first place.

The car fought through the downpour of rain which was strange for the time of year and seeing as it wasn't raining earlier in the day. When Cassidy reached out to try and clear it up, her abilities couldn't override it which meant that it was another Epsilon pushing the change. Despite her adrenaline pumping, the rain seemed to soothe her nerves more than she had ever anticipated. It was as if her own Origin was trying to prepare her for what she was going to experience in the coming hours, or even days. It was a future that was full of uncertainty.

Minutes seemed like hours, finally arriving on the outskirts of the Exodus conclave. It wouldn't surprise her if she was met with an entire army, ready to take her on and dismantle whatever coup she was considering throwing. It was obvious that the Exodus didn't want her harmed, since the Delta was surprised that she was even back in time. Was Chase supposed to distract her longer than he had? Cassidy had a million questions in her mind as she parked the car and headed to the back entrance. Seeing that it was left unguarded caused the pit in her stomach to grow. It was extremely unlike them to leave their outside forces defenseless, especially if they had anything to do with the League attack. This would've been the point that she assumed they'd be more apt to protect than ever before.

She pushed past the initial barriers, letting herself into the headquarters and heading towards the main hallways. The entire place was far too calm and quiet for her liking and it set her even more on edge than she ever thought possible. Something was out of place and it was taking her far too long to figure it all out.

The autopilot she had before was carrying her now, weaving around the corners to the middle hub of the Exodus. Who was it that she needed to find first? If she went to her father and he was somehow apart of it all, she'd have no way of getting out. If she went to find Chase first, it was almost guaranteed that he'd find a way to sink his teeth back into her or change her mind all together. But, if she managed to find out what happened to the League members who should've been in the Cove when it was attacked, she would have the edge. And, at this point, that was the only thing she had in her favor.

Standing in the center of the complex, she took in a few breaths to try and center herself. She needed all the help she could get at this point.

"Deep breaths, baby. You can do this. I know you can." A voice rang over her ears, Cassidy snapping her head around to try and pinpoint the direction it was coming from. Remembering the voice was easy, it was her mother. But, regardless of how the day's events played out, her mother was dead and would always be dead and that was clear so the voice she was hearing, she worried, was trying to trick her.

"Mom? How- you're not real," she said, shaking her head as she tried to push the thought out enough to focus.

"Cassie," she said, Cassidy's face falling when she heard the nickname that hardly anyone even bothered to call her anymore. It was apparent that the voice she was listening to was familiar but a part of her refused to accept that her mother could be speaking to her. "I'm gone, you're right. But, that doesn't mean I'm gone forever. This beautiful world, even you should be able to believe that I'm still watching, still keeping track of you growing up," she said softly, her words were warm even if they were only filling her head.

"Mom, I don't know what to believe anymore," she said, standing in the middle of the room a broken woman who simply wanted her mother to make everything right again; to patch the holes in her life that had just grown larger over the past half of a year.

"Oh, sweetheart, you do. You just need to think it through. Take a breath. You are so much more powerful than you can even imagine. I believe in you, Cassidy. I love you. I'll always be here." Her mother's voice was as soothing as it could be and she felt her heart rate start to slow, focusing on the breaths that she was taking. She needed to stay as focused on finding the left over League members and the only way she could do that was to use her abilities.

She stood centered, letting her breath come in and out of her lungs, trying to take what her mother said and use it in a way that could help her in this scenario. The green pulsed over her skin, spreading up her arms and over the rest of her body, eagerly trying to reach out through her Origin and solve the issue she found herself in. Turning to those inside the Exodus wasn't an option so asking another Epsilon wouldn't be useful to her and she was trying to desperately to avoid using her bond to pinpoint Chase's location. It was too dangerous to tap into it, only for him to turn it against her not only moments later. Sadly, this was a time that wasn't going to be solved using magic. It was going to be solved through simply working through the situation.

Cassidy walked down the hall to her right, spotting a few Chi security detail which caused her to hide back behind the wall she was pressed against. For her, she had already killed enough to last her a lifetime and if anyone else managed to see her, she knew that they'd want blood or to report her to her father. As she waited for the men to pass by, she managed to use her ability to distract them down another hallway, sneaking behind them and making her way towards the channeling rooms. The easiest way to weaken a captive person was to stick them in a channeling room for a different Origin and while she was still operating with the idea that they were still alive, that was the first place she was going to look.

It took a few more timely placed distractions to manage

to get close to the channeling rooms, hoping that they'd pick one opposite of Chi and Epsilon and settle on Sigma, knowing full well how emptying and deadening the Sigma room could be for anyone who wasn't Sigma. She had already assumed that she wasn't going to be able to find everyone all at once but she had to start somewhere.

She rounded the corner towards the Sigma room, nearly pummeling a Chi, the one that Jon had attacked over a month ago. It'd been some time since she'd seen him but it was clear that the two remembered each other.

"You shouldn't be out here, everyone is looking for you," he said, reaching out to grab her and she sent a strong wind gust, knocking him back about twenty feet or so and making him unable to snatch her up.

"Yeah? Well, they're gonna have to get in line. I'm looking for some people myself," she snapped, walking over towards him but he teleported before she had a chance to grab ahold of him. Before she knew it, he was behind her and his forearm was pressed against her trachea, trying to make her subdued long enough to take her in. Cassidy clawed at his arm, snapping her head back against his own which caused him to let go of her and before she knew it, she was sending electric shocks and then fireballs his way to get him to back off attacking her. Before she knew it, she caused the floor of the building to come up and capture his feet into cement and just as he was about to teleport out, Cassidy clocked him hard with her right hook, knocking him unconscious.

"Oh no you don't," she exclaimed, shaking the pain away from her hand as she finally stumbled upon the Sigma room. Her earlier distractions were enough to pull the sentry guards away except for two of them. The two men stood straighter when Cassidy made her entrance, trying a different approach than with the others before them.

"My father wants to see the two of you, I can look after the prisoners for now," she said, the two men Chis who seemed hesitant to accept what she was saying. It was then that Cassidy tapped into her bond with Chase, trying to see where he was and hoped that he'd be with her father. It took her a moment to recognize where he was but once she did and saw that he was on the right side of her father, she couldn't be happier about the fact that they shared a bond.

"What? Come on! They're up in the main choosing ceremony hall and it seems like they're pissed about something. So, get your asses up there and I'll be here when you get back. If, you get back," she said, crossing her arms over her chest, ready to strike if need be but the two glanced at each other long enough and moved out of the doorway and towards the main hall.

Cassidy let out a shaky breath, stepping to the door before glancing down the hall towards the Epsilon channeling room. She wouldn't have time to do both, sadly. It was either save the hostages—if they were still alive—or strengthen herself to survive what she assumed would be her last stand. Without another second, she opened the Sigma channeling room door, her feet carrying her forward enough to push her past the barrier and the instant sinking feeling revolted through her stomach. It was far more intense than she remembered previously but she swallowed back the subtle rumblings through her hands, focusing on whoever was inside the room. There were two people buckled and shackled to the floor, the smell of their flesh burning had managed to fill the room and was just as sickening as the feeling ripping through her stomach. Whoever designed the purpose of the channeling room was exceptionally brilliant. It'd strengthen one and weaken the other. The only person ever to be able to benefit from the rooms completely would be the person who could wield all five origins and despite what others spouted off to her, Cassidy wasn't that person.

It took her a moment to focus on the task in front of her, noticing the two men who were shackled to the ground. The first was Bryan, the Delta who also happened to be Cassidy's cousin. She was surprised that he of all people wouldn't be spared almost instantaneously seeing as he was related to the Chancellor but there was little that truly surprised her anymore. Everything she'd been fed over the past few months had culminated into one very large lie.

The second man who was imprisoned and chained to the ground was Sebastian. She'd be lying to everyone if she said that he hadn't found a special place in her heart. Of course, she'd argue until she was blue in the face that it was nothing more than a connection but many said otherwise. Regardless of who he had become, he was still Chase's brother and if Chase was enough of a monster to go to these lengths to get his way, the sickness in her stomach just continued to grow.

"Oh God," she finally said, moving to tear the chains away from them but before she could touch them, Sebastian cut her off with a groan.

"Don't touch them!" he breathed out, the searing pain etched across his face, Bryan's nearly mirrored. The chains had been on them long enough to burn off the first layer of skin on the men's wrists. It was a form of torture that she hadn't even seen before.

"Wh-what are they?" she asked, kneeling in front of the two, glancing over her shoulder every few breaths.

"They're Origin restraints. Keep you from using your Origin and only a member of the Origin who placed them can get them off without harm," Bryan breathed out, noting that it was a Sigma who placed the chains originally. It was smart, at least, for the Exodus to use the Sigma Origin, knowing that there weren't many of them in the first place so finding someone within the League to help was few and far between. She just hoped that Yvette and Caleb were as safe as they could be somewhere else within the compound.

"Okay, but, we don't have time for this right now, someone will be coming soon," she said, watching as the men tried to avoid moving even a fraction of an inch if only to spare themselves from the pain. It was obvious they'd been in the room long enough to feel its effects so even if they didn't want to move, even if they focused all their energies on keeping still, the Origin withdrawals were enough to keep them shaking. With each movement, the shackles shifted and seared into a new piece of flesh. It was an ingenious torture system but a horrific one.

"Just go," Sebastian breathed out, taking in a sharp breath before lifting his head to look up at her. "Run. Find someone to help you break your bond, break your connection to the Exodus and keep running." It was obvious that Sebastian was on the edge of giving up completely. Losing his sister, losing his Origin, falling down a path of destructive behavior only to be pulled out of it and to lose the stabilization he'd worked so hard for... he was done. It was a look that Cassidy had learned from him over and over again and being the woman she was, she just pushed him that much harder. One more step, one more breath, one more was all it took to realize the pain you felt is manageable. It didn't matter that he wanted to give up because there was one thing that Cassidy Hawkins would never do and that was give up.

"If you think I'm going to let you be the only hero today, you're wrong," she teased with a gentle laugh, moving to slip behind both of them, staring at the blood soaked iron shackles. She knew that using her own Origin was practically a death sentence. Standing inside the Sigma room and using her Epsilon Origin would drain her faster than anything else she ever experienced. She wasn't terribly strong as it was but she was going to try her damndest.

"Cassidy—" Sebastian started, shifting to move away from her which caused a muffled scream to roll through his throat. She placed a gentle hand on his shoulder and sighed.

"Stop moving, give me a minute," she scolded, turning to Bryan first and touching the shackle as if she was a puppy testing the limits of a shock collar. The burning sensation erupted through her skin, the skin turned a bright red but didn't bleed just yet. "Fuck," she muttered, swallowing her pain for a moment before looking the lock over once more, grabbing at the bolts that seemed to be holding it closed and yanking as hard as she possibly could while swallowing back her screams. Her fingers had started to bleed and she could hear the metal shifting but not enough to get it to break. Just as she was about to take her hands away and think through another strategy, Bryan took in a quick breath and yelled, adding his strength to the mix and it only took a few tough tugs to get the metal to fall from his wrists. It clattered to the ground and Bryan turned, wanting to rub his wrists but he refrained to avoid harming the open wounds. Cassidy ripped a part of the bottom of her shirt, allowing him to wrap up the wounds as best as he could.

"Your turn," she muttered, moving to Sebastian as she squeezed her hands closed, pushing through the pain as best she could. She could tell that Sebastian didn't want her to get him out of the shackles, almost hoping that Bryan was strong enough to do it for her but Cassidy could tell that Bryan needed a minute for himself to push through the waves of feelings overwhelming him at the moment. "I'm going to need you to push against them," she said softly with a grimace, swallowing as she stared at the shackles once more and moving to pull against them. The cacophony of their screams blended together, Sebastian's wrists bleeding more than they were earlier but after a few moments, the shackles clattered to the ground and Sebastian was released, the man falling forward on the ground as he buckled in pain. Cassidy ripped off two strips from the other side of her t-shirt, it now short enough to reveal a small portion of her stomach if she moved in a particular way. She slid them to Sebastian to cover his wounds as she wiped her own blood off on her t-shirt. When she wiped her hands on herself, she started to realize that she could feel the negative effects of being inside the room, the Sigma energy slowly but surely starting to try and take over her own. "I know you two need time but we don't have much of it and we need to get out of here," she said, looking up at Bryan who had managed to get to his feet. Sebastian was now on his knees, also working to get his feet underneath him as Cassidy did the same. Both men nodded in response to her comment, taking shaky breaths as they headed towards the doors.

"Do you guys know whe—" she started as a Sigma member rounded the corner, the orange energy fresh on his fingers. Cassidy took in a sharp breath, ready to defend them but before her Origin even managed to hit her fingertips, Bryan sent out a large black bear surrounded in silver Delta magic and the bear quickly lunged for the man's throat, ripping it open before the Sigma had a chance to get a shot off. Bryan's legs buckled at the lack of strength from exerting himself, Cassidy quickly slipping under his arm to help him in the hall where the bear absorbed back into Bryan's frame, the man's blood pouring out on the floor.

"You didn't have to do that," she whispered, helping Bryan to a chair and frowning, looking up at Sebastian who was already standing sentry, pacing slightly. Bryan reached out and touched her face, managing a gentle smile and it was obvious that the two had the same smile. Cassidy's own lips turned into a grin when she realized the trait they shared and listened as the man spoke.

"I did. I'd do anything for you guys," he said, swallowing back the shakiness in his voice before looking over his shoulder for the Delta channeling room. "You guys go find whoever the hell decided to do this, I'll get the others and we'll… meet somewhere." Cassidy didn't like the idea of separating but he was right. Just like before when Cassidy was thinking through her options, there wasn't enough time to find the person who attacked them and save everyone who was taken. It was feasibly impossible. If they found their attackers, they'd deal with them while the rest of the group managed to off the survivors. If they found the hostages, the people who did this would manage to get away with attacking them in the first place. The only way to get justice and everyone to safety was to go in two groups. It wasn't perfect but it was the only solution.

"You be careful, alright? I didn't just save your ass to have you go get killed," she teased, leaning forward and giving him a hug, burying her face against his chest for a moment before releasing him. She hated herself for not giving him more time in her life, knowing that he was some of the only blood she had left.

"Don't worry, you can get to know me like I know you once this is all over," he teased, tapping her on the top of her head before turning on his heels and heading deeper into the compound, away from where the Chancellor was holed up.

It was at this point that she turned to Sebastian, moving to stand next to him and letting out a terrified breath. The next few hours of her life were going to change dramatically. The was no more benefit of the doubt. No more convenience. People were dead because of her ignorance and her inability to believe what was right in front of her. She wasn't going to allow that to happen twice.

"I'm sorry I didn't believe you," she said softly, staring down the hall in which they needed to go, refusing to look up at him. Sebastian did the same, standing in a way that he had more than one vantage point, shaking his head.

"I know you better than you think, Cassidy. I don't think I've ever been able to convince you of something without you seeing it for your own eyes. I'm sorry it had to come to this but, I'm just glad you believe me now," he said, taking his eyes off of the hallway for just a moment to gaze down at her. Cassidy's confusion was clear, licking her lips to question him but he shook his head. "You can ask me later, okay? When we're safe, when we're whole, alright?" She wasn't the only person to lose people in the attack and at the moment, all he could think about was getting everyone out in one piece.

"They're up in the main hall. I saw Chase there with the Chancellor. My bet is that most of them are there and that only guards were left to watch over you all until you either died or proved useful." She frowned. "You sure you're up for this?" she questioned, watching his reaction and Sebastian's look spoke volumes to his answer.

"I've never been more ready," he said, the red sparking violently over his hands and the two walked down the hallway.

Chapter 22

J don't understand why we didn't just kill them," Chase said, standing next to a desk and the Chancellor was staring out the window towards one of the courtyards. There were a few Chi guards in the room but many of the other Exodus members were either protecting their assigned places or simply told to believe that they were safe in their rooms. It was obvious that the willing army that the Exodus had hoped for was slowly but surely showing their want to have a free will but that had yet to stop them.

"Because," the Chancellor spoke, not bothering to look over his shoulder at the man that had become his protege over the years. "We've been far too hasty tonight as it was. Wasting all of that pure Origin blood would be for not. Not when we can make them prove themselves and become useful again," he said, clasping his hands together as he continued to stare outside, watching as the sentries changed various stations as the minutes ticked on. Chase let out a huff, moving to sit in the chair across from the desk, putting his feet up on the table as well. It was Chase's call to go in and round up the League while he had Cassidy distracted. It was also his call which resulted in the deaths of those from both factions. While he hadn't anticipated deaths, he also told them to use whatever means necessary to round up the traitors. He preached to the men in his ranks how revolting the people they were going after were to the Exodus and how much their betrayal could bring about the end of the life as they knew it. Chase was far from an idiot. While he could stand there, hands clean from the blood that he brought, he got others to do the dirty work that he stood clear of. His charm and charisma was enough to seal the deal.

"You say that like they're worthy to come back. Look at Cassidy. It's clear that altering someone's memory will only work as well as it can but that the host will eventually win." Chase sighed but the Chancellor simply laughed.

"Or you weren't nearly as convincing as you hoped that you were," he said, causing Chase to rise to his feet, the red sparking over his fingers. The man had a soft spot for Cassidy, that was apparent, but he knew the job that he needed to do. Win over her heart, win her from the members of the League and get her to break them from the inside. He'd managed to win her heart but obviously lacked when it came to the other aspects of his mission. He had argued the danger of putting her with people that could trigger true memories from her previous memory trail but the Chancellor had assured him that it would all work.

"Or maybe your daughter isn't the one you think she is and this is all one big show for nothing," he growled, the Chancellor reaching back and grabbing him up by the throat and hoisting him into the air. Chase clawed as the man's hand, the red sparking over his hands which got a laugh and a snapping of the Chancellor's tongue. Chase subsided his Origin attack, still clawing at the man's hand which was slowly but surely sucking the life out of him.

"Never, ever, say a bad word against my daughter, again, if you hope to live another day," he said, his voice eerily calm as he released Chase to the floor, the man clamoring to rub his throat, the cough spreading from his lungs. If he were honest to himself, he would admit how strange it was for someone who was so appreciative of his daughter and treat her the way that he had.

"Whatever you say, boss," he said, coughing as he rose to his feet, clearing his voice as best he could as the two guards who were guarding the Sigma room came in, interrupting the two of them.

"What the hell are you two doing here?" Chase said, glancing from the guards to the Chancellor and back to the guards once more. It was clear that the guards were starting to doubt Cassidy's story that she had told to get them to be moved in the first place.

"The girl, sir, your daughter said that you wanted to speak to us," one of the guards said, straightening his back up as he spoke as if trying to seem taller than he was. Chase narrowed his eyes at the admission, frustrated that Cassidy had managed to get through the defenses that he had set up.

"Seriously? You're far more gullible than you look," Chase said but it was only seconds later that the Chancellor was walking to the men, standing in front of them with a calm smile before speaking.

"So, she's here, I take it? Unharmed?" he questioned, glancing to his fingers before the men continued.

"Uh- yes sir. We were outside the Sigma room before we left," he said, clearing his throat and the Chancellor reached out, grasping his hand around the back of his neck before grinning even more than before.

"Thank you, for your service," he said, his index finger shining a bright silver color and transforming into the end of a scorpion stinger, injecting the poison into his throat. The paralysis set it almost instantly, the Chi sinking to the ground and blinking up at the ceiling as the venom started to take over. "The Sigma room, that was Ezekiel and your brother, correct?" the Chancellor asked, pulling his handkerchief from his chest pocket, wiping off his fingers and acting as nonchalant as he possibly could. Chase stood in slight disbelief as he watched the man under his command twitch on the ground from the scorpion venom.

"I thought you said no more Origin blood was to be spilled," Chase remarked, disregarding his question.

"He was fooled and far too easily. I do not want that weakness in my home," he said with a shrug. "Now, answer my question."

"Yes," Chase said begrudgingly, looking towards the courtyard to see if he could spot them coming to meet with them. "We have to assume that she knows everything, if not now then soon. She wouldn't be pulled to him first if she didn't know," he said, rubbing the back of his head, trying to think through what was going to happen once she got there.

"Fret not, dear boy. Have more faith in your bond. Even if she was meant to be with Sebastian, this Cassidy has chosen you over him many times. Remember that, use your Origin if you need to but keeping her with us is what matters far more than anything else. I assure you," he said, glancing to the other guard who had failed to keep his post. "And you, do you need to meet the same fate as your friend here or have you learned to keep a better head about you?" he asked, tilting his head as the guard scrambled to his feet, shaking his head emphatically. "Right then, on you go. Go clean up the mess you decided to make," he said, sending the guard out of the room and glancing over to Chase who was suddenly tapping his hand against the top of the desk as a nervous tick.

"She'll be here soon, we know she will. She's too strong headed to think otherwise. Our plan is solid. Settle down, Chase," he said, clapping the man on the back and squeezing hard, Chase having an odd sensation roll up his spine at the thought of where the Chancellor's hand was in the same position, killing the man who was trying so desperately to scream out as the venom continued to take over his nervous system.

"And if it's not?" Chase asked, glancing over to the Chancellor, trying to read his face as the man answered. "Are you going to have your daughter killed?" he asked, swallowing while he separated himself from the Chancellor, gazing back into the courtyard.

"There are less extreme ways of handling her. That's what you're here for. Regardless of how this night ends, she'll be on our side. Whether or not the members of the League, including your brother, survive tonight will be dependent on how Cassidy plays through all of this," he said, continuing the nonchalant rhetoric he had adopted over the course of the night. Chase wasn't too keen on the thought of yet another member of his family dying for the cause but he'd rather them die for this than to die in vain.

Chapter 23

You know we might have to kill them both," Sebastian said, the two weaving in and out through the corridors, trying desperately to get to the Chancellor and Chase as quickly and as safely as they could. Cassidy didn't even bother to look over to Sebastian when he spoke, trying to stay focused on the task at hand.

"You don't have to remind me, Sebastian," she cautioned, sliding up against the wall and peering over it, inching her way down towards the next place she could hide up against for protection.

"But, I do. I can hear your heartbeat escalating when I talk about it. If this plays out how I think it will, this will end with either us dead or them." Sebastian spotted an Omicron member walking the halls, teleporting behind her and seaping the red energy into her skin to get her to fall asleep, helping her body to the floor in the process. Cassidy's arm was still stained with blood from killing the man back at the League but she was trying so desperately to avoid killing anyone in the night's events. Much like the Chancellor thought, this wasn't the time to be killing so many people in their community. The only way she was going to get people to come together would be to unite them, not drive a farther wedge between them which is what killing would continue to do.

"I'm not going to admit that there isn't anything within either of them that's redeemable. I helped you come back from the edge, I can help them understand it too," she said, allowing Sebastian to lead for a few moments. His head hung low at her words, a sharp intake of breath at what she said and he simply chuckled, shaking his head.

"The fact that you can even compare what I've done to what they've done to us, to our people, to you? How can you even assume that they're saveable?" he asked, turning to look her over, his face echoing his disbelief.

"You killed me, remember?" she snapped, blinking up at him and watching as his face turned even more sour at her words.

"You to—" He stopped, biting down on his tongue and taking another deep breath. "You know, you're right. I did. I ran you off a road, forced you to trigger and didn't make it to you in time to join with you. And, while I'm sorry I did that to you, I'm not sorry for everything else. I'm not sorry for being here, for worrying about you, for trying to get you to see the purpose and the truth that you're so desperately seeking. Now, your dad and my brother did this to me," he said, showing her the blood soaked shirt rags that were wrapped around his wrists. "Jane is dead. Not including whoever else was killed. For all we know, your own cousin is dead back there because he gave himself up to help us get here. Look at your arms, Cass," he said, pointing to her hands but she refused to look down. "Look at them!" he said, grabbing them and shaking her forearms so that she had to snap out of her own head to pay attention to him. "Cassidy, this, you killed tonight. That sinking pit in your stomach that you're feeling right now? I know how that feels. Fuck, I know what that pain tastes like better than anyone." He swallowed, squeezing her arms until she looked up at him, licking his lips as he watched the terror and hatred and pain swell up within her.

"I love him," she said, the tear falling over her eyes for a moment before she took in a stumbling breath. "And, he's my Dad," she added, the break in her voice happening in the middle of the word Dad. "What am I supposed to do right now?" she asked, moving her arms so that she could clasp his, avoiding the wounds on his wrists.

"You are the strongest person I've ever met. And right now, you're going to confront them and take it one step at a time. That's the best advice I have for you," he said, trying to not let the hurt show on his face at the fact that she said that she loves Chase. "We have to get moving, though. If Bryan survived long enough to get to the others, it's only a matter of time until others go to help them," he warned, squeezing her arms once more before turning to head back down the hall that he was originally leading down. Cassidy tried to push all the thoughts running rampant throughout her head, begging and pleading with the internal struggle that was going on within her to settle long enough to get through the night. Sebastian was right and she knew that but it wasn't as simple as just accepting the truth and moving on. This truth brought up issues with two men whom she thought she could trust with her life. She just hoped that when she reached them and found out all the truths that she would be happy with them.

It only took a few more minutes to move into the outer foyer to the main hall. Cassidy's heart was beating loud enough that she was positive that everyone in a five mile radius could hear it pounding against her ribs. Her blood flowed excitedly throughout her bloodstream, eager to prepare her body for whatever was behind those doors that were in front of her. It seemed as if the past six or so months were meant to culminate to this moment, at this time. She couldn't look past her terror and excitement in the moment but if she were being honest with herself, she would admit that it was all an orchestrated mess and one that she would get her father to explain, once and for all.

"You ready?" Sebastian asked, glancing over tentatively before Cassidy nodded, grasping the door handle and pushing it open, moving into the entrance of the doors as if she owned the place, her gaze landing on both men simultaneously. It took everything in her body to hide the quick gasp of air that was a natural reaction to spotting them both. The impulsive reaction to seeing Chase pulled at her body, desperately trying to bring them together when all she wanted to do was to keep her feet buried in place. She wanted to stand strong and listen to the truths that Sebastian had just told her but their bond was nearly suffocating her. Her body gave in slightly, moving a few steps closer to Chase to which everyone in the room noticed and it caused the Chancellor to manage a smile.

"Hello, darling, it's nice to have you back home," the Chancellor said, his voice even more soothing than ever before, practically drawing her in just the same as Chase's bond was doing. Cassidy blinked a few times, trying desperately to quell everything that was hitting her senses all at once. To say it was overwhelming was an understatement. Sebastian noticed Cassidy's unnatural reactions, moving steps closer to her, even if she was trying to distance herself from him. "And you brought home our lost Williams brother as well! Your father would be proud to see you back in these walls, son," he said, changing his focus to Sebastian who narrowed his eyes at him.

"My father would be turning over in his grave to see Chase and me here. I just hope that by the end of this, no Williams blood will be in these halls anymore." Sebastian moved, still within protective range to teleport Cassidy out if need be but he was putting himself farther forward to anticipate an attack faster than Cassidy could. At this moment in time, he wasn't too sure of her attack skills towards the two men in front of them.

"Now now, no need to be hostile. Besides, Chase is here on his own free will," the Chancellor said, glancing to Chase and then back to the pair before resting his eyes on Cassidy, moving to take a step towards her.

"Take another step and we're gone," he warned, gritting his teeth and Cassidy placed a hand on his shoulder, moving to stand even with him and gave it a gentle squeeze.

"It's okay, Sebastian. I can handle this," she said, releasing his arm and switching her gaze between Chase and the Chancellor, chewing on the inside of her lip as she tried to figure out where she was going to start first.

"You destroyed their home and... killed innocent people for what? To get peace? I had it covered, I had a way out! You two, betrayed my trust, lied to me, and hurt my friends in the process!" she said, her voice escalating as her own truth came out. Sebastian would be lying if he said he didn't know of what she was doing while in the League. It was obvious that she didn't severe her ties with the Exodus after everything for a reason and the best reason was to be spying on them all. Almost the entire group knew it but allowed it to happen simply to win Cassidy's trust, which they had. "You messed with people's minds and after everything... how could you do that?" she asked, swallowing back the pit in her stomach.

"This is so much bigger than all of us, Cass," Chase said, stepping closer towards her which got the red energy sparked over Sebastian's hands. Chase shot a look to his baby brother for a moment before looking back to Cassidy. "We didn't have time. What Yvette did, attacking humans, nearly killing them and exposing us in the process, we had to bring everyone in for questioning. It wasn't our intention to hurt anyone! Those who were killed attacked us first, we just defended ourselves. Cassidy, you know me, you looked me in the eyes and asked if I had anything to do with helping Yvette attack those humans and you said it yourself that I was free and clear. Why won't you believe me now?" he said, looking the woman over and

Cassidy blinked a few times, trying to sort through it all. She hated it when he tried to make sense of all the issues that were going on in her head.

"Don't- just, stop trying to use our bond, Chase. Get out of my head and just—" She paused, taking in a breath as she shook her head. "I don't believe you anymore. You used the blind spot I have for you and you exploited it. I can never trust you again," she said, the pain in her stomach welling up as the words escaped her lips. Despite how much she begged to believe him, despite how much she needed to believe him, she couldn't. Not anymore. The final breath that Jane took wreaked havoc through her memories every single second she closed her eyes. And, never would she allow herself to just sit idly by and watch as someone she cared for died because of her blindspots.

"Cass, come on. You're gonna believe them over me? After everything? I love you," he said, taking another step towards her but Sebastian was there, the red intensifying in his hand. Cassidy pulled him back, taking a step towards Chase and the pain was clear as day on her face when he uttered those last three words. It was as if he took a knife and dug it into her side, the agonizing pain ripping through every fiber of her life. The redness burned across her chest, the adrenaline spiking through her blood as she stared at him.

"I'm going to believe that assuming everything is a coincidence is naive," she said softly, taking in a shaky breath and nodding her head. "I've been so clouded being with you that I never saw it. I could've prevented Jane dying. Or, from people getting hurt... I could've saved everyone so much trouble if I had just never fallen in love with you," she said, biting down on her lip to stifle any more tears that begged to break the surface. "But, no more. You've violated my trust and my mind. How could I possibly get past that?" she asked, glancing from Chase to her father for a moment before returning her gaze back to Chase.

Chase watched her reaction, hoping that the words that

left his lips were enough to reel her back in but it was clear that that wasn't going to happen in the moment. Maybe if Sebastian wasn't there but with the man protecting her from every little thing, there was no way that he was going to be able to reign her back in to their team.

"Darling," the Chancellor piped up, clearing his throat for a moment before continuing. "Now, I'm sorry that you've lost a friend or two tonight. We managed to lose some too, in case you were curious, even at your hands as I've been told," he said, pointing at her dried bloody hands. "I'm not going to yell, as there is no point to it, but you need to understand what we were trying to do tonight. Exposure is a risk to all of us, regardless of what faction you side with. We were attacked when we got there this evening and we did what we thought was best for all parties. Now, I'm sorry some of your friends were killed in the process but that was always part of the deal. You were there to provide information and intel on how the League worked, how it was set up. You provided the interworkings for tonight's raid and if it weren't for you, we would've had no idea how to get in, let alone get in successfully. You made it so that we can protect this family that we've created, to make us all better and stronger and your sacrifice was not made in vein, darling. I promise you that you will be stronger after this." The Chancellor's voice almost made Sebastian get on board with what he was saying, it was so soothing. Something about it simply made you want to agree and nod and just continue on. It was probably that reason that they were so able to get everything they ever needed.

"Cassidy, don't listen to them. This was their plan all along. You were trying to find your place," Sebastian said, taking a step closer to Cassidy once more but the woman wasn't having it.

"He's right though, Sebastian. I'd go and report to them every few days. What happened tonight was because of me, because of everything that I told them," she said softly, trying desperately to not think so terrible of herself but she couldn't shake the feeling. Sebastian glanced back towards her for a second and shook his head, distracted long enough for Chase to use his ability to throw him clean across the room, far enough away from Cassidy.

"Sebastian!" Cassidy cried out, the action snapping her out of her downward spiral of dark thoughts long enough to snap her to the present. Sebastian was crumpled on the ground, moving to stand but Cassidy already had the green energy burning against her skin, a bright red ball of fire barreling towards Chase. The fire caught the arm of his sweater, Cassidy taking steps back towards Sebastian as she was ready to counter anything he tossed her way.

"Enough!" the Chancellor bellowed, staring between all the parties involved before looking to Chase. "Enough of all of this." Chase calmed, the red subsiding from his skin before laughing softly, the confusion spreading across Cassidy's face.

"Oh what? Confused, gorgeous? I'll admit, at least you were pretty. And powerful, I'll give you that but dealing with your insecurities and all your issues was exhausting. How in the world he managed to do that for years still boggles me," he said, nodding towards Sebastian and Cassidy's confusion continued to grow.

"What are you talking about? What's- what's going on?" she demanded, staring at all three men in the room with her.

"Are you meaning to tell me that he had all this time but never really told you how he knew you? Before our dad went all scrambled egg on your memory?" Chase asked, watching the both of them for a response before laughing even louder, clapping his hands at the site. "Oh, brother, come on. Too afraid to hurt your precious little prophecy over there?" Chase's words seared into Sebastian and the man, who was now on his feet, nearly growled at his statement.

"Chase, don't. She doesn't—none of that pertains to this. Leave her mind alone," he spat out but Chase just laughed again, shaking his head proudly.

"Oh, no, this is prime time to have this talk. She might not remember all of it anyway, depending on how this all plays out so, why not at least know now?" he teased before turning his attention to Cassidy, teleporting behind her and grabbing her arms up, red hands pressed one against the side of her temple and one to her stomach. Cassidy squirmed to move away, the green magic pooling around her hands before Chase spoke.

"Ah ah ah, sweetheart. I promise you I'll be faster in your head than you'll be harming me, and you'll just harm yourself in the process," he said, speaking softly into her ear which caused a shiver to spiral down her back. "Now, where were we? Oh yes, Mr. Moon-Eyes over here," he said, teasing Sebastian who was ready to pounce the second he saw an opening. "You see, he and I have been triggered since we were kids. We've known this life since we were young and while that didn't matter much to others, it did matter when it came to you. You weren't apart of this world in an Origin sense of the word but everyone knew who you were. You are Cassidy Hawkins, daughter to Elizabeth Hawkins and Xander Hawthorne, protege to taking over the reigns as Chancellor should you ever be triggered. So many people had opinions on that but, Sebastian over here, whew," he said, pulling her back against him a little harder as he spoke. "He fell madly in love with you years ago. And, before anyone could really put a stop to it, you two were together." Chase paused when Cassidy processed his words, gazing to Sebastian who looked so hurt that she was finding all of this out this way.

"Bingo! You two were two peas in a pod, or, at least until your good 'ole mom had to go and be incredibly unuseful. See, we were told by a pretty powerful Chi that someone in your bloodline, someone close to the Chancellor would fulfill the prophecy and wield all five origins. We swore it was your mother and the Chancellor tried to figure if it was her but, she just couldn't take it all. So, when the magic he was feeding her ended up killing her, what else could we do but make you all forget it!" he exclaimed, burying his nose into the smell of her hair, closing his eyes for a moment before lifting his head to continue his story. "Losing you was enough to put this one in a disgusting spiral of using and abusing and despair and then when he came upon Holly forcibly triggered by the Chancellor to start building his army, it was only a matter of time till we framed him, stuffed him in the League and continued on with our plan. It took us a while to get all the details ironed out but, once the League was able to track and recover you, we just slipped in after Sebastian managed to get you killed and the rest, the rest is history." Chase's voice was smug, that was clear, clearly happy with himself that he helped execute such a convoluted plan. Cassidy continued to squirm in his arms, practically begging and pleading to be released from his grasp.

"Why?" Cassidy asked, trying to slip down out of his grasp but Chase bent with her, picking her back up into his arms and holding her hostage.

"Why? Because, if it's not you who fulfills the prophecy, we'll just go down the list. Eventually, it'll happen and the minute that it does, we'll make that person a weapon and help us ascend to greater heights than ever before. No more hiding. No more waiting in the shadows, no more watching humans get everything we want out in the open. From that point on, our future is no longer questionable."

"And you think I'm going to help you guys... after all of this?" Cassidy said, still trying to pull herself from his grasp. Chase grinned, leaning his lips closer to her ear as he spoke, his breath warm against her skin.

"You love me, remember?" he said, his voice low but still loud enough for everyone in the room to listen. "Besides, all it takes is a wave of a hand and you won't remember anymore of this, just like last time. Who's to say we haven't been through this a few times already? How can you even trust your own mind now?" he asked, spinning her in his arms, forcing her to stare into his eyes, the red pulsing over her skin and it was clear that she started to melt into his arms as he whispered to her.

"Don't! Chase! Cassidy, don't listen to him. I promise you, don't listen. You can fight whatever it is. You're stronger, I know you are!" Sebastian cried out, watching as Cassidy nodded at Chase, her back still to Sebastian. She spun on her heel, walking towards him and Sebastian went to teleport but Chase shook his head, staring as Cassidy walked.

"Move and I'll take away every memory she has all the way back to age five. She'd literally be a walking toddler, capable of doing pretty much nothing until she learns it all from me, your call," he shrugged, the red spiking over his fingers as he watched the scene unfold.

Cassidy continued to walk, watching Sebastian and he was quickly pleading with her, hoping and praying that he hadn't already wiped her memory.

"I know you don't remember us. I wish I was strong enough to help you then like you've helped me. Cassidy, I've been lost without you. Whatever you want to know, I'll tell you. I'm sorry I didn't do it before but I didn't want to scare you away. Please, Cass, look at me. You know me. You know how I feel. Whatever Chase said you have to do, you don't. Fight it, you're strong enough to fight anything," he pleaded with her, watching as Cassidy finally crossed to where he was standing, quickly pulling him into her arms and pressing her lips against his. He hated his initial reaction of wrapping his arms around her, knowing that there was a purpose in sending her to do exactly that. A few other thoughts swam around his head, thoughts of teleporting out of there, attacking the two men and knocking her unconscious long enough to get her to safety... all of the thoughts were valid but her sanity was too delicate to risk. He knew just how desparate Chase would get if need be and risking her memory wasn't something that he wanted to do anymore.

"I don't understand," he muttered, setting her back to the ground when their lips pulled apart. It wasn't necessarily how he wanted to kiss her again but it was far past the time in which he wanted to do it. He knew it came with strings, though. Never would Chase grant him the joy of a kiss. As Sebastian thought on the matter, the knife that Cassidy used to stab herself, the one that was collected from the League in the raid earlier in the evening found a new home in Sebastian's back, piercing fairly deep and causing Sebastian's knees to buckle, the pair clattering to the floor. Sebastian stared into Cassidy's eyes which were glazed over and obviously coerced into doing something that she simply didn't want to do.

"He said you'd want a taste of what you'd never have again before you die," she said with a shrug, as if she just told a child that they weren't going to be able to have ice cream since they didn't finish their dinner. It was scary and eerie, the tone of her voice as she pulled the knife out, setting it to the floor next to them as Sebastian clamoured his hands behind him in an effort to stop the bleeding.

"Cass, I need your help, please," he muttered, Cassidy conjuring up Epsilon chains which were just like the Sigma ones he had on earlier but the woman snapped them on his wrists before he had a chance to move, keeping him bound there. Sebastian screamed, the metal reopening the wounds that were at least scabbing over from earlier. Sebastian really was backed against a wall, the pain from both wounds starting to sear into every aspect of his body. The Chancellor and Chase stood clear from the pair, their smiles more smug than ever. It was clear that this was their endgame all along. If Cassidy wasn't truly the person to fulfill the prophecy, they were going to see to it that she became a weapon of some sort, whether she wanted to or not. It took months to truly break her, to put her in a place where it didn't matter the history she had, the subtle feelings she could've had for Sebastian; the only thing that mattered was her loyalty and her ability to jump when told to do so.

"I told you your bond was nothing to worry about. See?

She's cooperating beautifully," the Chancellor said, clasping Chase's back in excitement before moving to the two on the ground, Sebastian's blood pooling underneath him enough to create a puddle.

"Cassidy, don't listen to them," Sebastian said, coughing up blood as he watched the Chancellor get closer, his hands covered in his own blood as he desperately tried to reach out to her, to grab her hands and get her to remember anything. The chains burned against the fragile flesh that they were touching and his teeth gritted against one another to stop himself from screaming. All he could try to do was push past the pain and hope that Cassidy was in there somewhere.

She pulled her arms away from Sebastian's reach, moving to stand to welcome her father. It was still unknown as to what Chase told her that made her so compliant but it was obvious that it was working. The man opened his arms up for her, pulling her into a hug which she welcomed just as quickly as he did.

"Welcome home, my darling. We have all missed you. And with you here, without any more distractions or reservations, we'll be the strongest we've ever been," he said, pushing her hair behind her ear as he gazed over her face.

"Of course, Father. This is where I'm meant to be," she said calmly, lifting her lips into a smile as she received him in the same manner he did for her. The air in the room was so strange as the three standing seemed to be conversing as if nothing else was going on but Sebastian was clearly dying on the floor at their feet. He moaned out in pain, writhing on the floor and reaching out to grab either of them, the chains clattering against the marble flooring. When he was rolled over, his eyes locked onto his brother's, the hurt obvious in his eyes.

"Chase, don't do this. Don't follow in his footsteps," he choked out, trying whatever he could to get someone in the room to see reason. Instead, Chase walked to close the space between him and the other two, happy to see Cassidy not only calm but apparently happy, regardless of all the blood on her.

"Cass?" he said, waiting for Cassidy's attention to fall upon him as he grasped her hands, giving them a gentle squeeze. He was hoping that what he was about to say wouldn't need any coercion but he'd use it if need be. "I know you've had a long day. But, right now, I need you to do one more thing for me, can you do that? For us?" he asked and she glanced from her father back to Chase and nodded, licking her lips in anticipation. "That's my girl," he said sweetly, reaching up and touching her cheek, the smile growing on his face before he went on with what he needed. "You did a great job with Sebastian here but, I'm afraid, it's too dangerous to leave him here to just die and his strength is too vast to just waste. I'm going to need you to channel his energies. I'll be here the whole time if you need me, I promise," he said, gesturing down to Sebastian who was a large puddle of blood at this point, trying to scoot back away from the three as he heard what Chase needed her to do to him. With the amount of blood that he had lost, the pain and torment he'd already gone through and the amount of his Origin that he managed to use already in the evening, he knew that it wouldn't take her long to practically snuff the magic and the life right out of him. It wasn't a common action to do, especially for one that wasn't in Sigma but channeling was a process that was generally mutual. Normally, someone would push a little out, take a little in and learn to control their abilities that way but it could also be used to the extreme if one was powerful enough. Cassidy only had the control of one Origin, she was exceptionally powerful with just those abilities and it was clear that she'd be able to channel in a way to get what she wanted, especially if coerced to do it.

"Cassidy, fight this," Sebastian spat out, the edges of his vision slightly fuzzy but he was pushing through it if only to try and save her one final time. She looked from Chase to her father who pushed her to continue on Chase's orders, moving to kneel next to Sebastian. It was the first time she'd looked at him after she stabbed him, her eyes glancing from the knife and to the man who was writhing tremendously in pain. Before she even moved, she just stared at him, taking in the sound of his pain, the look on his face, the way his blood was starting to fill the little crevices in the marble underneath them. There was a subtle nagging feeling in the back of her mind that made her want to think this wasn't how the night was supposed to end, that it was supposed to end in a different way all together but she couldn't put her her finger on it just yet.

"Should I help?" Chase asked, his hand igniting red and the Chancellor tugged him back, shaking his head.

"This has to be her. You've set the precedent, you gave her the parameters, she has to go in for it now or we'll be making these calls for her the rest of her life," he said, almost sounding as if he was watching his child learning how to ride a bike without training wheels instead of committing murder. No matter the free will that Cassidy still had, it was clear that the original coercion that Chase set forth was still in her mind, chugging on as truth as the green slowly erupted around her skin. Sebastian saw her Origin, letting out a gutwrenching breath and closing his fists when he could finally tell that she was going to carry out Chase's order.

"I don't think it'll hurt," she said, her fingers brushing up against his arm before she managed to clasp against his, linking her fingers in line with his own. The green Origin flashed a brilliant green color, igniting over her skin and into his as his skin started to burn a bright red. The chains kept him from being able to use his Origin but it made it far easier for her to take it from him.

The cry that left his throat nearly pierced the windows in the room, his fingers digging into the backs of her hands as he felt the energy from his Origin being transferred into her. There were times before that this act was done voluntarily, while Sebastian was relearning control and simply trying to stay afloat with his Origin. Cassidy and he had nearly daily sessions until he was able to shoulder the ability he had cultivated over the years. But this had a completely different feel than before. Instead of being consensual, he could feel the energy being ripped from his body and siphoned into Cassidy's. Instead of her calming voice ensuring that he was alright and that he could handle it, Cassidy simply sat there, the green of her Origin glowing brighter as the seconds ticked by.

"I love you," he whispered, Cassidy finally looking down into his eyes and noting just how green they were. They were just as intense as the first time she could remember meeting him in the bar, before she ever knew who he was. As the Chi Origin energy surged through her body, she could feel her strength growing, the catch in her breath causing her to snap her eyes closed and her nose was bleeding before she even had a moment to notice. As the origins blended together inside of her and her eyes were pinched closed, all she could do was think which took her deeper within herself than she ever had been before.

With the Chi energy surging in with her own, her closed eyes transported her back to her dream she had over a month ago of chasing her mother through an endless maze, nearly a second behind her. She weaved eagerly behind her, calling out and pleading with her to simply stop so that she could catch up to her. By the time that she did, unlike before, it was as if Cassidy was watching a memory, rather than a dream.

"Xander, I'm begging you, keep Cassidy out of this. You let her go, you leave my little girl be," Elizabeth pleaded, the woman kneeling in front of the Chancellor, her hands shaking violently and the color was drained from her skin. It was clear that the effects of Origin overuse was running rampant through her frame but she exuded a strength that was unmatched by most. Regardless of the pain that was evident among her body, she was still putting up a hell of a fight.

Xander crossed the short space between him and the

kneeling woman, grabbing her face and hoisting her gaze up towards him so that she was looking at only him. "She is my daughter too, must you forget. Whatever I say goes when it comes to her. If she gets triggered tonight, tomorrow, it will happen when I deem it is a good time. Not a minute earlier or a minute later, do you understand?" he snapped, letting her face go and Elizabeth kneeled strong, not bending or cowering or even trying to move away from his grasp. Every single inch of the woman who was kneeled on the ground exuded a kind of confidence that Cassidy remembered, or at least she thought she remembered. Watching the scene unfold in front of her started to nag at the back of her head, continuing the thought that what she was replaying was in fact a memory, not a dream.

"You see her as property. As a pawn in your game to rule the world! I will not let you take her from me. No matter what you may think, whatever you think you can convince her of, one day, it will all come back to her and there will be no one there to protect you from your decisions. I may not be the one to bring you down but damnit, I promise you, it'll come," she said, spitting up into his face in aggression. Elizabeth, being one of the most powerful Chis around was generally respected when she promised something in the future. One of her many gifts was the telling of not only prophecies but seeing the future in general. And, knowing that information, Xander smacked her dead across her face, the anger swelling inside of him simply left unchecked for too long.

"You fool! You are leaving this home we've built for a bunch of degenerate disgraces to the name of our origins! Here you will have power beyond measure! Here you will achieve greatness and I will make sure you get there!" Xander said, almost as if he was trying to convince her, through everything, to stay. Elizabeth laughed, her tongue sneaking out to the edge of her lip to lick away the blood that he had brought to the surface, shaking her head.

"You lost me the second you used my own Origin against

me. How long did you think feeding me other Origin magic was going to last until I broke? Look at me! Xander!" She paused, trying to stand but the weakness in her body refused to bare the weight of her. "LOOK AT ME, DAMNIT!" she screamed, Cassidy now no longer in the room but hiding behind a door in the hallway, the door leading into the room that Xander and Elizabeth were in. Instead of seeing the entire dialogue, it was clear that Cassidy was now reliving what she actually experienced over a year ago. These were the memories that were wiped from her.

"You loved me once. Even if you refuse to admit it to yourself. Because, underneath the man that is in front of me right now, there was once a man who had beautiful ideals, respect, honor. He wasn't a man who would take away someone's identity just to get what he wanted. Your hunger for power has made you disgusting and as much as I wish I could pity you, I can't," she said, still kneeling upright but the rest of her body was trembling uncontrollably.

"I'm sorry you feel that way, Liz. I really am. But you know what I'm most sorry for? I'm sorry that you are completely invaluable to me now," he said, his voice cavalier as he delivered what was practically a death sentence to her. Before she was even able to get another word off, the Delta magic swelled from his hands, the silver Origin burning into Elizabeth's skin and sinking in. To someone so overwhelmed with magic consistently over the past few weeks, it was hard to shy away when the magic started to creep within her skin. It was just as addictive as a long time sober person tasting drugs again for the first time in years. The trembling stopped as Elizabeth's body accepted the magic, her eyes changing from the pale blue to a deepening black until her pupil spread over the entire color of her eye. Before she could even take another breath, Xander was pressing more and more magic into her. Elizabeth could tell it was too much, trying to pull away but her body's natural reaction to want more overroad her fight or flight instinct.

"If you hurt my daughter, I'll find a way to end you, even in the afterlife," she said, a cry leaving her throat as her body began to shut down. Cassidy pushed open the door, stumbling into the room as the silver magic started to dissipate and her mother's heart stopped beating all within the same second.

"Mom!" she cried out, running to her side and shaking her, begging anything or anyone, whoever would listen, to not take her mother from her. She clawed at her body, pulling her up into her lap and trying to nuzzle herself into her hair. "Mommy, please don't leave me, please," she cried out, the tears soaking Elizabeth's shirt as the woman's color left her face. Cassidy waited a few more breaths before looking up at her father, blinking away the tears that quickly turned to absolute hatred for the man in front of her. She heard everything he had to say. Hell, she saw most of it.

"How could you do this, Dad?" she spat out, clutching Elizabeth's body to her lap as if trying to protect her, even though it was too late.

"Darling, it's not what it looks like. Your mother, she was sick, sh—"

"I heard you, Dad! Fuck, I saw you! You... you're a monster! You killed my mother! And you have the audacity to stand here and lie to me when her body isn't even cold yet!" she bellowed, laying her mother on to the ground and clamouring to her feet, wishing now more than ever that she had an Origin of her own to command.

Xander's eyes narrowed, shrugging his shoulders at her accusations. Regardless of what she believed, he knew that he could convince her, much like he originally convinced her mother, to trust and believe in him. And, the best way that he could do that was to be joined to her. Before he said a word, he moved and had her lifted off of the ground, his hand clenched tightly around her throat and hoisted into the air. Her scream echoed through the room as he pressed her against the wall, his grip strengthening as she fought against him. Her nails dug against his skin, clawing and ripping at his hands as they tried valiantly to save her own life. She knew that it was a moot point but she would be damned if he could kill her just to get what he wanted.

"Dad," she croaked out, her skin turning a bright red and slowly working its way into the purple spectrum as her body begged for air. Her hands started to claw at him just a fraction slower and she knew that she'd be unconscious in the next few seconds.

And, with that realization, Sebastian had opened the door, hearing her screams further down the hall and the sight of the woman he loved being killed by her own father, Elizabeth sprawled out on the floor, it was evident that he happened upon the scene just at the right time.

"Cassidy!" he yelled, the red Origin sparking over his hands and knocking Xander clear across the room, pulling Cassidy into his arms as the woman took a few deep breaths, rubbing the skin around her throat.

"Go, go, go," she said, patting his chest and before she knew it, she was spinning through a teleportation back to Sebastian's room. The room was much like his that he'd create in the League but it was evident that she was living there too. Her clothes, her things, touches that were evidently female instead of male and the rooms were littered with photos of the two of them together.

"What the fuck is going on?" he asked, pulling Cassidy into his arms and trying to sort through the mess that he had walked in on.

"He killed her," she said, the realization settling in even more, now that she wasn't in the room anymore. "Bas, he killed my Mom and and, tried to kill me," she said, rubbing her throat and trying desperately to figure out what to do next.

"We have to leave," Sebastian said, moving to the closet and grabbing up an already packed up duffle bag, ready to go at a moment's notice. Things in the Exodus had been rough for some time, especially after Elizabeth left the group to begin with. Sebastian and Cassidy weren't originally planning on leaving at all but they wanted to be prepared for the worst, in case it happened.

"No, we can't leave," she said softly, watching Sebastian's realization when she said that she couldn't leave. "He killed her, Sebastian. He killed her in cold blood. He just tried to forcibly trigger me and we're the only thing that can bring him down. Don't you get it? This... this is what the League needs to win this fight before it even begins!" she said, the drive in her voice clear as day as she stared at the man she loved, the bright purple bruise spreading over her throat, clearly in the shape of handprints.

"But—you, you're human, Cass. And, you are one hell of a fighter, you just can't hold up in these kind of fights. We agreed weeks ago that if it came to this, that we would run because having you safe, having us together... was worth more than anything else, remember that?" Sebastian closed the distance between them and slung the backpack over his shoulder, staring at her. The bruises on her neck caused a pit in his stomach to grow, watching just how vulnerable she could be in all this.

"Then trigger me!" she exclaimed, opening her arms up. "If anyone should do it, it should be you. I want you to do it. Screw what my mom has been saying for years, this is my choice and I choose you. Do it, Bas. Kill me and bring me back and not only will I be stronger but we'll be stronger. We'll be joined. We can do this," she said, and the fear practically escaped from her as she spoke. The adrenaline was carrying her through her words now, marching her on from sentence to sentence.

Sebastian was taken aback by her statement. They'd joked about it once before but Elizabeth was so adamant for her to experience the trigger naturally that no one, not even Xander, dared forcibly trigger her despite the years she spent within the Exodus. Of course, now that she was dead, there was no one to stop Cassidy from doing what she wanted to do in the face of the most ultimate danger. Her father.

"Are you sure about this?" he asked, brushing her hair back and moving down to press his lips against her forehead, sighing heavily.

"There's not a person in the world that I trust more than to do this. We'll grab a bag, go someplace out of the way and we can do this. Train a bit, hook up with the League and then plead our case. It's us. It's me. The Elders will believe me. I won't let him get away with this. Please, Sebastian. I need you," she said, looking up at him with the redness still clear in her eyes. The pain was obvious and he could tell that it was going to take some time for her to heal but he was more worried that her entire decision to trigger herself was fueled by some need for revenge against her father. At the end of the day he was still her Dad but he'd oblige her, if only to get her out of the Exodus, out of harm's way and into safety. Maybe once there was distance, she'd think clearly enough to want to stay out of the world that inevitably killed her mother.

"If you want me to do it and are sure... then, let's go before there's no way for us to leave, alright?" he said, moving to grab her hand when the door to their apartment ripped open, a man making his way through promptly grabbed Sebastian up and pulled her away from Cassidy.

"Dad?" Sebastian said quickly, noticing that it was his father that had entered his room. Before he knew it, his father was seeping the Chi Origin into his body, slowly making him woozy.

"I'm sorry son, he threatened your mother and Holly, I had no choice," he said softly, watching as Sebastian crumbled to the ground, unconscious. Cassidy screamed for help, trying to run past him when he snatched her up, craddling her body against his.

"Shh, I'm not here for him. Well, I am, but I'm going to do my best to give you as much time as I can but, I'm sorry. This... won't work if you remember. I trust that the love you have for my son will guide you two back together. You two were always meant to be, no matter who tried to keep you apart and no amount of Origin magic can get in the way of that. So, I'm going to do my best to hide you. But, one day, you'll be brought back here. One day you'll be forced to relive the horrors that you've faced tonight and for that, I'm sorry. Your mother asked me to protect you if anything happened to her and this is the best way that I know how, Cassidy. So please, forgive me one day. When you remember this, when you have to see how this night played out, all I ask is for your forgiveness." Chase and Sebastian's father, Richard, seeped his magic into Cassidy's body, blocking out her entire life as she knew it, filling in the holes where necessary, creating an entirely new life and family, a new history devoid of the Exodus and of Origin magic. She was to live her life as a normal woman until the time came to bring her back and show her what she went through. And, because of his blatant disrespect to Xander's orders that night, Richard was murdered by the Chancellor the next night.

It only seemed like a second past in the real world while Cassidy's mind remembered what happened that night, her body continuing to syphon out the Chi energy from Sebastian as she sat there, kneeling. She couldn't remember anything before the day that she just remember, it was as if the Chi Origin that was seeping into her skin was unlocking only fragments of her original history which surprised Cassidy entirely. Everything that she'd been told about regaining her original memory was useless since Richard Williams was killed. Cassidy couldn't pinpoint what caused her to suddenly remember the evening but she was thankful for the clarity, nonetheless.

When Cassidy opened her eyes, she could see the short, rapid breaths that Sebastian was taking as he struggled to keep his heart beating as the Chi Origin was being stripped from her. The realization of that night was enough to break hold of Chase's own commands as she began to take in the surroundings and all the exit strategies. Controlling how she channeled from him, she made it so that it looked like she was still taking from him, the green spark of Epsilon magic igniting brighter every other moment or so to make it look like she was growing stronger. It didn't take but a second for Sebastian to notice it, trying desperately to lift his head to look her over but he couldn't. She shifted her weight, moving her non-linked hand to the chains that she had shackled on him a few moments earlier. As quiet as she could, she tugged on them, freeing on the hand that was hidden from the Chancellor and Chase. Using her own Origin magic, she used the opportunity she had to spark the electricity in the next room over, causing a bright explosion of light and a rather loud popping noise to distract the men from what she was doing. Her free hand went to the wrist of Sebastian's linked hand, freeing him from that one as well and once both of his wrists were freed, her hand went to his chest, tapping excitedly.

"Go, go, go," she said, her words nearly echoing exactly what she said when her father tried to kill her that night. Sebastian blinked at the realization that she had somehow broken free of Chase's hold long enough to free them both. Mustering up the last of his energy and feeding off of some of Cassidy's, the two snapped out and teleported out of the room, only to infuriate both Chase and the Chancellor at losing the pair.

Sebastian managed to land them roughly ten miles outside of the Exodus, in a rather open but brush filled clearing. The two clattered to the ground as it was obvious that they'd pushed their limits on how much Sebastian could stand.

"Bas," she said softly, clinging to his body as he tried to lay there, still writhing in pain and losing blood rapidly. She couldn't remember anything about their relationship other than the night that she got while channeling from him but it showed her that at one point in her life, she trusted him with her life and then some.

"You remember," he said softly, looking up at her and

cracking the best bloody smile he could muster, all things considered.

"No- I mean, yes, I remember some things, but only that night, nothing more, really," she said softly, squeezing his hand and looking around at where they were. She had hoped by now that the others that were captured had been rescued, pulled out and tended to. And, she hoped more, now than ever, that she could get ahold of one of them. "You just rest, okay? I'm going to get help," she said, giving his arm another squeeze before moving a few spaces away from him and sitting down. She mumbled a few words, pointing in a five star order in the same order she would if she were organizing the origins to get into the League compound. It took her a few moments, trying desperately to do it by herself which was only something she had seen someone do, never attempted herself. After a few seconds passed by, Joseph and Flora arrived a few feet away. The two were just as roughed up as others. Their wrists were obviously healed but the scars were evident that they were shackled just as Ezekiel and Sebastian were.

"Oh, thank God," Flora said, looking from Cassidy to the ground in which Sebastian was laying, the man barely holding on at this point. "What the hell happened?" she questioned and Cassidy hugged her arms to her stomach, trying to figure out what to say happened.

"Long story but please, help him. He's not doing well," she pleaded, moving over with Flora and watching the blue Omicron Origin surge over Sebastian's body. Cassidy's eyes darted to Joseph, ready to talk to him while Flora worked.

"We need to leave. Is there anyway you can teleport us while she works on him? The Exodus are going to be looking for us, now more than ever and if she doesn't treat him now, he'll die," she said, swallowing back all the emotions she had experienced over the night. Joseph nodded, moving between Flora and Cassidy and placing a hand on both of them as Flora's hands were on Sebastian. It took a moment to get going but within a few seconds, the group was teleported back to the makeshift League headquarters. The building was large but rather plain, much like the last time. They had an emergency switch that got them through all of the security locks in one fell swoop instead of having to take the time to go through each and every one of them like they did before. Once they were on the inside of the sanctuary, Cassidy took in just how lucky she was that she wasn't nearly as beat up as the rest of them. All of the survivors had burn scars around their wrists from the chains, and in one room a small group of dead bodies had been recovered including Jane's from earlier in the night and one that appeared to be Geneva.

"Geneva is dead?" Cassidy exclaimed, looking to Joseph for answers as he nodded.

"When we were trying to escape, she had to go back for one more once they were freed. A Chi ended up getting her before she even had a chance," he said softly, shaking his head. "Numbers are still a little rough but it looks like five dead, three unaccounted for, or well, one now. The rest of us are pretty rough but nothing the Omi's can't fix for us," he managed, looking Cassidy over, staring at her bloodied hands.

"It's not mine," she managed to say, rubbing her hands along the tattered fringe of her shirt, her eyes darting around the room to try and find if Bryan managed to make it out. "And Bryan?" she finally asked, peering around to try and find him.

"Well, prior to you two getting here, he was the worse off out of all of us. He's resting in one of the side rooms. Some of the more stable have been trying to set up Origin rooms but it takes up far too much energy and most of us are beat," he said with a nod, Cassidy trying to take the night's events in. With Geneva gone, the entire League would be scrounging for a leader and from what her last memory of her mother was, that seemed to be a role she was destined to fill.

"No, no, you're right. We all need to rest. Heal up, take a breath where we can and just start on rebuilding tomorrow," she managed to say, only directing her gaze to Flora when she popped up from helping Sebastian.

"Is he going to be okay? Please, tell me he's going to be okay," she mumbled, chewing on the inside of her lip as she waited for Flora to answer her.

"He's pretty rough, I'm not going to lie. It's going to take him some time but, he'll pull through. And, I'd say it looks like he has you to thank for that," she said, moving to grab her hand, squeezing it gently before Cassidy muttered out a thank you. A few others went up to her, feeling a need to check up on how the events of the night played out for her and Cassidy asking the same. It was nice to see that even though everything that happened, they all still seemed so connected. She knew that it was time to break her bond with Chase and with Epsilon but it'd have to wait for daybreak for that to happen. For now, she'd simply work on staying vigilant through the night so that Chase didn't happen to use that bond against her.

Her feet took her to the side of the bed that Sebastian was resting in, her hand lying on top of his as she sat in the empty chair. The voices around her were all rather hushed, people thanking one another for helping the other survive. It was clear that this was the family that she originally thought that she was fighting for. It was the one that her mother before her had fought to have and she wished that it was clear to her back then as it was now. So much bloodshed and lives could've been spared if she'd had just known what all was going on.

"I'm sorry I haven't... I'm sorry I'm so stubborn," she said to Sebastian who was still unconscious. "I should've known from the moment I met you who you were to me. And, although I can't remember anything before that moment between the two of us, I know what you did for me that night. Your father gave up his life to ensure that I'd have a chance in this fight. I'm sorry for everything that I said and did and God, if you'd had died tonight because of me..." She trailed off, wiping away the tear that was rolling down her cheek, burying her face into her hands as she took in a shaky breath. "All I know is that now I know what I'm fighting for. I'm fighting for my mother. I'm fighting for your father. I'm fighting for you. I'm fighting for all the people surrounding us tonight that put their lives on the line for this cause but most importantly, I'm fighting for me. Because, all I want to do now is make my mother proud of me and you know what? I'm sure we can win this thing. This is war," she said, her back standing a little straighter in the seat as she watched Sebastian take in a few shallow breaths, the bright red Chi Origin conjuring to Cassidy's hands for the first time ever. Finally, she was able to wield a second Origin.